The Hidden Wife

B.M. Hardin

This book is a work of fiction. All persons, events, places and locales are a product of the others imagination. The story is fictitious and any thoughts of similarities are merely coincidental.

<u>Dedication</u>

This book is dedicated to all of my loyal and dedicated readers! Special thanks to my book group and readers "It's A Book Thang". Thank you all for your support and for following me on my writing journey. It is truly a blessing to have supporters like you in my corner. Thank you!

Acknowledgements

First and foremost, I want to thank my Heavenly Father for my talents and my gifts and each and every story that he has placed in me. It is an honor and a privilege to be living my dream and walking in my purpose and for that I am forever thankful.

Also to all of my family, friends, critiques, supporters, readers and everyone else, thank you for believing in me and allowing me to share my gifts with you.

Your support truly means the world to me!

B.M. Hardin

Author B.M. Hardin's contact info:

Facebook: http://www.facbook.com/authorbm

Twitter: @BMHardin1

Instagram: @bm_hardin

Email:bmhardinbooks@gmail.com

TEXT BMBOOKS to 22828 for Release updates!

THE HIDDEN WIFE

Prologue

"I vow to love, honor, and obey you. For the rest of my life. As long as we both shall live. I'm yours and I'll do anything to make sure that we make what we have, last forever. I'm yours. Now. Tomorrow. And forever more."

I don't know about other women, but when I said my vows, I meant them. Things haven't always been easy for us. But since we were eighteen years old, I've had his back, and he's had mine. And all we have is each other.

****

CHAPTER ONE

This had to be some kind of joke!

There was just no way that this was the man that she'd set me up on a date with. I mean, I just had so many questions.

Like why is his head so damn big? What 90-year-old woman did he steal his chin from? Why is his nose pregnant with twins? Why do his lips look like day old hot dogs? And where in the hell is his neck? I mean, did he leave it at home or something?

I closed one eye and leaned my head to the side. Nope! He's still ugly! My blind date was so ugly that a baby passed by our table, looked at him and started to cry. Poor baby. I feel your pain. Hell, he scared the hell out of me too when I first saw him.

What in the hell was my sister thinking?

He smiled at me and I threw up in my mouth a little bit.

"Darling are you okay?"

"Yes, I just need to go to the bathroom," I said, excusing myself from the table. I walked slowly, and just before turning the corner, I glanced back to see if my blind date was looking in that direction. Seeing that he was now looking down at his phone, instead of going to the bathroom, I hurried in the opposite direction, towards the Exit sign.

I am going to kill Shelly! I smiled as I had of small vision of me hitting her with my car, reversing, and then running over her body over and over again. She knew better than this! How dare she send me on a date with somebody's overgrown pet?

Once I was home, I called Shelly, my sister, in hopes of giving her a piece of my mind for setting me up with *Donkey Kong's* first cousin, but of course she didn't answer. She was more than likely, cuddling with her husband and their new set of twins, while I was snuggling under a blanket, all alone, about to devour a pint of ice cream, since I'd skipped out on dinner.

Bitch.

I knew that I shouldn't have trusted her to find me a date. She'd always had a thing for unattractive men. And her husband was no different. He had been beaten with the ugly stick too. Thank goodness for our genes or the twins would have been ruined! But since Shelly had spoken so highly of Coby, my blind date, I thought that I would give it a try. But never again.

My problem was that I didn't know how to date. My ex-husband and I parted ways two years ago, after an eight-year marriage, which we'd dated two years before that, so I have been out of the game for quite some time now. And before meeting my husband, I was young, and sexy, so I wasn't interested in anything serious. I was just throwing booty in different directions to either satisfy my needs, or to get something that I needed.

So now that I was divorce, I had no idea how to find love or how to put myself in a situation for love to find me. Even the first time around, I hadn't been looking, my ex-husband actually pulled me over for a traffic ticket, and the rest is history.

Ray, my ex-husband, and I hadn't gone through a nasty divorce or anything. When we got married, we were crazy in love with each other. We had so many goals and dreams. The good part was that we both accomplished everything that we'd set out to do, but the bad part was that somewhere along the way we forgot about each other. As years went by, we simply fell out of love with each and fell in love with money and our careers. My career took off before his and I always felt that he was intimidated by me making more money than he did, so gradually he just seemed to resent me for that too. But finally, after years of holding on, we agreed that a divorce was the best thing for both of us and so now, two years later, I was still single, but I was hopeful.

If I could just get out there, I could definitely get a man. I was sure of it. I was a damn good catch and I had a lot to offer. I was attractive, smart, independent, successful and a little on the freaky side too. I had a few extra curves but that was nothing that a good girdle couldn't fix. I just had to learn how to stay out of the office, and get on the scene.

I flipped through the channels until I came across a dating chat-line commercial. I listened to the woman talking and eyed the actors as they pretended to be in love and happy. The number flashed across the T.V. one too many times, and I picked up my phone.

I mean, chat line dating was in these days…right?

I'd heard so many success stories and I even knew a few folks that had gotten married to people that they'd met online or over the phone. I guess you could find love anywhere, as long as you were looking.

So, I placed down the ice cream and dialed the number. After only a few minutes of following instructions and then listening to a few male callers, out of nowhere, a bell chimed in my ear.

"Someone wants to connect with you. Press one to chat live with the caller. Your future husband is waiting. Press that button," the automated woman said as I pressed the number one. Here goes nothing.

"Hello," he said, in a husky, somewhat intimidating tone. "So, this is my first time on here. I don't really know what I'm doing," he confessed. I took a deep breath.

"Me either. I'm Strawberry," I introduced myself.

"Is Strawberry like a real name or a stripper name or something?" He joked and I surprised myself by giving him a sincere chuckle.

"It's a nickname that I've had since I was a little girl. Of course it's pretty self-explanatory. I loved strawberries as a child and well, one day my grandmother called me Strawberry and I've been stuck with it ever since," I explained.

"I like strawberries, they're sweet and juicy. Hopefully you are too," he said just shy of a whisper. I was a little out of the game so I wasn't sure if he was innocently flirting with me or being a pervert, but I tried not to think too much about it.

"So…" He started to say but then another voice spoke.

"Hello? Jimmy, I need the phone. I need to call and check on my prescription. This yeast infection is killing me! Could you go pick up my cream for me if it's ready? You know I dropped it off at the 24-hour pharmacy over there on Broad Street. I can't wait until morning. I'll be up scratching all night!"

Wait a minute…what?

"Ma, hang up the damn phone!" he screamed.

"Who are you talking to like that? Boy, I'll come up there and---,"

I hung up the phone in a hurry but immediately regretted it once I did. I should have stayed on just to listen. I started to laugh, so hard, for so long, and it felt so good! I hadn't had a good laugh in a very long time.

Well, I would take that as a sign that my Mr. Right was just going to have to find me the old-fashioned way. And hopefully he was already on his way.

~***~

"Who is it?" I yelled as I headed towards the door.

"Ray."

Ray? My ex-husband Ray?

It was funny how he'd just crossed my mind the night before and all of a sudden, out of nowhere, he just pops up. Of course he knew where I lived, since he'd given me the house during our divorce. But since the day that he moved out, he'd never been back. Not even once. So I was surprised that he was here now. After the divorce we'd tried to stay in touch as friends but it had been well over a year since we'd last communicated with each other. I guess we both just got busy and after all, I wouldn't say that it was exactly healthy to text or talk to your ex-spouse every day.

I opened the door and he smiled. I hadn't seen him in person since we'd signed the divorce papers, even though we'd talked a few times after that. But boy did he look good! He'd always been attractive but for some reason he looked better than ever. His presence caused a hundred memories to flood my mind and heart all at once. For some reason, I had the dying urge to lick his face.

"Uh, Ray, what are you doing here?"

"You were on my mind, and---" He didn't finish his sentence and before I could ask another question, Ray walked closer to me. I studied him. He seemed nervous.

"Wait, what are you doing?" I questioned Ray as his hands touched me. His touch made me weak. I hadn't been touched by a man, in over two years, so I was well overdue, and my *kitty* purred as a reminder.

"Do you ever think about us?" Ray said, still caressing my outer thigh. Wait. This must be a dream. Yeah. I'm just feeling a little lonely and thinking about old times. I closed my eyes, but when I opened them, he was still there.

"Ray, I don't know what you want from me but…"

"I want you to say that you miss me too," he said and as he finished his sentence, he kissed me. At first I was in shock, so I didn't kiss him back. But that didn't stop him and soon my lips started to move, even though my mind was telling them not to.

What are we doing? We're divorced.

My mind was racing and all over the place as he pushed me back towards the couch and kicked the front door closed behind him.

What happened to hey, how are you doing? Can we talk for a minute? I haven't seen you in a while, how have you been? Are you seeing anyone?

What happened to all of those questions?

I wanted to tell him to stop and be logical, but he seemed to be having some kind of outer body experience or something. The way that he kissed me, and touched me, was as though he was hungry. As though he had been thinking of coming here, and doing exactly this, for quite some time.

"Tell me that you miss me," he whispered as he tugged on the bottom of my dress.

But I didn't miss him. I think. Or at least I didn't until he showed up. At that moment, and because everything was happening so fast and sort of strange, I didn't really know what to feel. The only feeling that I was able to recognize was that I was about ten steps past horny.

My vibrator was my best friend but there was nothing like the real deal. But I had a feeling that if I told him, just what he wanted to hear, that I was going to get lucky. Maybe most wouldn't screw their ex-husband, who they hadn't seen or heard from in forever, but I was about to and I was going to enjoy it too. I could write this off as some kind of booty call, or something and be completely fine with it being just that. At least he wasn't some random man that I'd met at the bar or something. At least I knew him. And if he was passing out penis, I'd might as well let my vagina enjoy a stroke or two.

"I missed you."

At the utter of my words, Ray's eyes lit up and what came next was pretty much a blur. We rolled around from the couch to the floor for over an hour. It was exactly what I needed. Exactly what I wanted. And it was good! We'd always been good in that department, but it was definitely better than I remembered.

As we both laid there, breathless, I tried to get my thoughts together. I didn't know whether I should tell him thank you or to put me down for another round next week. I just wasn't sure.

What happens now?

Ray stood up and I covered myself as though I hadn't just allowed him to touch every part of me.

"Um Ray, what was that? Where did you come from? Why did you come here?"

He continued to get dressed before responding.

"You've been on my mind. I guess I was just feeling…I don't know. I guess I missed you Tiffany," he said calling me by my real name.

I didn't know what to say. I mean I wasn't seeing anyone and obviously he wasn't either. Maybe we could start over. Or maybe we could at least screw from time to time.

"I don't know what to say. Do you want to stay a while so that we can talk?" I asked him, and he looked at me as though he was filled with sadness; either that or as though he was constipated. I couldn't quite tell.

"Sorry. I can't. I have to go. I'm late for my bachelor party. I'm getting married in the morning. Bye

Strawberry," he said and walked out the front door, leaving me with my mouth hanging wide open.

What the hell did he just say?

~***~

"Girl, you know that was wrong."

"What? There is nothing wrong with Coby. He's sweet. And he makes a lot of money. I thought that the two of you were going to hit it off," my sister giggled.

"Shelly, did you not see the way that he looks? I wouldn't even let him smell it. If I'd looked at him too much longer, I was going to need counseling. Hell, you know I already have a problem with nightmares," I said to her.

Shelly laughed long and hard, but I was serious.

"Well, what about your boss?"

"Who Al? He's married."

"So."

"So...he's off limits. What is wrong with you Shelly? I'm sure you would die if Brian was fooling around on you," I chastised my sister for her remark.

I was still in a bad mood about Ray coming to my place and having sex with me, knowing that he was getting married the next day. He used me. And if I could have found the church that he was getting married in the next day, and believe me, I looked, I would have given him and his "was going to be" wife, a show that neither one of them would have ever been able to forget. I would have cursed him out so bad that I was sure that she wouldn't have married him. But lucky for him, none of the six churches that I went by, were having a wedding that day.

Yet, knowing that he had really moved on and that he was getting married again really made me feel some kind of way inside. It really had me thinking and I even felt like a failure in a way. Not in life, but in love.

Why couldn't that have been me? Why couldn't I have found someone new? I wanted to be in love too. I wanted a second chance at happiness too.

"No I wouldn't. Hell, if Brian fooled around on me, it might actually help a sista' out a little. It would surely take some of the extra work off of my hands. Can you believe that he thinks that he's supposed to get sex every day? Like every single day? Who has the time to do that? I mean, I just can't. After work and the twins, I'm exhausted. If I could have it my way, once a week would do me just fine. But every night, his ole begging ass comes tapping me on my shoulder for some booty. I tried to play dead a few times, but that never works. He just climbs on top of me and starts pumping anyway."

I laughed from the pit of my belly. My sister was always so over dramatic about everything. Here she was, complaining about her husband wanting to touch her when I was yearning for a man to want to touch me.

"It's not funny Strawberry. I'm not about that life. A bitch be tired! But I gotta' trick for him tonight. As soon as he starts tapping, I'm going to reach for the bottle of lotion on the end table and hand it to him. He and that lotion gonna have a good ole' time tonight. I might even join in with a sound effect or two. Maybe that will help him out."

"You are a mess."

"But I'm serious."

"Did he find a new job yet?"

"NO! And he's been looking like crazy too. He hates that I'm paying all of the bills but I'm holding everything together. Hopefully he gets one soon."

"I told you, I can give you some money. No loan. I have plenty. I can give you a few thousands, that you can have, until he gets back on his feet."

"Girl, no. You already do enough. You already pay all of Mama's bills and you're putting April through college. I'll be fine. Besides Brian would have a heart attack if you gave me money and if he knew that I'd been telling you everything about our finances. Hell, his own Mama doesn't even know that he lost his job. We will be okay."

Just as she finished her sentence, there was a light tap on my door and I motioned for the janitor to come in so that she could do her job.

"You're still at the office aren't you? Tiffany, it's almost 7 o'clock. You're never going to find a man cooped up in that place all the time," my sister said. She's right.

"I know, I know. I'm about to go. I'll talk to you later," I said and hung up before she sparked up another conversation. Within minutes, I gathered my things and finally headed out of the building.

I worked for a multi-billion-dollar design company where we designed underwear, lingerie, and swimwear for hundreds of other companies. All of those cute little flowers on panties, or that bra with hot pink lace with leopard print, or those cute high-waisted two piece swimsuits that women love to wear so much, more than likely was the idea of one of our designers. And then brands, companies, buy them, place them on their products and sell them.

I was the V.P. of Sales and Marketing, and I made the big bucks. I'd worked my ass off to get to that position but had I known that it was so lonely at the top, I might've headed in a different direction or at least put a little more effort into my marriage.

I twirled my briefcase and my small Gucci bag as I headed to my car in a hurry. I frowned at the sight of the flat tire on my driver's side.

"Damn it," I groaned. How in the hell did that happen? I took a closer look and saw a nail. I must have run over it on my way back from lunch.

After calling roadside assistance and hearing that they weren't going to be able to make it to me for another two hours, I hung up the phone, stepped out of my 6-inch heels, pulled my weave into a bun and took off my blazer. I popped my trunk and found my jack. I was just going to have to change my tire myself.

Of course I knew how to change a flat tire. I was the daughter of the best damn mechanic that ever lived. Daddy had been a mechanic and though he'd had three girls, he always made us help him in the garage. He'd always said that it was good for us to know how to do things for ourselves, you know, just in case a man wasn't around to do it or in my case, if there was no man in the picture at all. I could change a flat tire, change my oil, replace spark plugs and there were a ton of other things that my father was able to teach me before he died. To be short, work had killed him, literally. A 1985 El Camino fell on top of him while he was working under it, crushing his insides. He worked day and night, doing what he loved, but thinking about it now, I was a lot like him. And that wasn't exactly a good thing.

Shaking away the thoughts, I grabbed the jack and prepared to get down to business. But...

"Hey, do you need some help?"

I shielded my eyes from the late evening sun and followed the voice.

He towered over me and extended his hand to help me off of the ground.

"I was riding by, and I said to myself, what kind of man would I be to let a beautiful woman change her own flat tire? Not on my watch. Excuse me," he said and stepped in front of me. He started to unbutton the ivory colored suit jacket and unloosened his ivory, red, and navy blue tie.

"Hold this for me," he said, handing me the jacket and his watch.

A Rolex. And it was real.

Hmm...somebody has some money I see.

He got down on the ground and got to work. As he examined the tire, secretly, I examined him.

He was tall; well over 6-feet. He was also a little on the skinny side; not too skinny where he could be blown away by a nice strong wind, but he was definitely a lot smaller then I usually liked my men. But he had big feet and big, strong hands…and he wasn't wearing a wedding band.

Checkmate!

The shape of his eyes were intriguing, and not to mention that they were a light, noticeable brown. They complimented his skin perfectly, which was smooth and chocolate like rich and creamy cake frosting. I smiled as I gazed at his head full of soft, black curls. And he had one dimple, on his left cheek, that popped up every time he turned the handle on the jack. He was definitely something good to look at and if I could stare at him all day long, I would. I won't even mention the other things that I would do to him if I could.

"Thank you so much for doing this for me. I really appreciate it."

"No problem," he grunted as he tightened the lug nuts on the spare.

"I'm Tiffany by the way. But family and friends call me Strawberry."

He glanced at me and smiled at the word Strawberry. Nice smile. Hmm…I'm definitely coming on to him.

I didn't know if I still had the magic words like I used to, but I was about to find out.

"I'm Tobias. And you Ms. Strawberry are all done," he said slapping the tire, and lowering the jack.

"How much do I owe you?"

"Don't insult me," he said with just a little authority. "You don't owe me anything. Just get that spare off as soon as possible and get home safely."

"You wanna go home with me?" I said aloud accidentally. Sure, I had been thinking it but I damn sure hadn't meant to say it. I hurriedly covered my mouth in embarrassment.

"I did not mean to say that," I muffled through my fingers.

Tobias chuckled and surprisingly walked closer to me.

"Are you sure you didn't mean to say it?" he asked slyly.

I smiled and so did he. He looked at me as though he wanted to say something. I was hoping that he asked for my number.

"I tell you what, how about I treat you to dinner? We leave your car and go to that nice little Southern spot down the street. I mean, I'm sure going to your house would be a little more entertaining, but I'm not easy…you have to earn this," he joked as he placed on his jacket and his watch. He has a sense of humor? I like it.

"Really? So, you're asking me on a date?"

"I mean we both gotta eat right? If you don't want to go, that's fine."

"No. I would love that," I said to him in a hurry, before he could change his mind. After placing back on my shoes and with my car all locked up, I turned back to face him.

"Okay, let's go."

We headed across the street to his Hunter green Land Rover. He opened the passenger side door, but just before he shut the door he spoke, "So, Strawberry, I guess it's safe to say that you're a little freak huh?" Tobias laughed hard, and slammed the car door as I blushed and buckled my seat belt.

Humph. If you play your cards right, one day you may get to find out. But this time I just thought it and didn't say my comment aloud.

✳✳✳✳✳✳✳✳✳✳✳✳✳✳✳✳✳✳✳✳✳✳✳✳✳✳✳✳✳✳✳✳✳✳✳✳✳✳✳

Chapter Two

"Are you sleeping with my husband?" she asked, inviting herself into my office, closing the door behind her. I recognized her. She was my boss's wife. She was his second wife since I'd been working with him. Their marriage was fairly new, and personally, I liked his old wife better. I didn't really know this one, and she wasn't all that friendly.

Al, my boss, was the only person above me in the office. Sure there were folks above him, the owners of the company and all of that, but on a daily basis, it was him...and then me.

Now yes, he was fine as hell. Had he not been married his little Spanish speaking, taco eating ass would have gotten a taste of all of this a long time ago. But he was married and I didn't do married men. So, as far as I was concerned, he was off limits.

"Sorry, you must have me confused."

"Hmm, Tiffany, I don't think so. You see, last night, he called me your name...while we were having sex."

My mouth open, but I closed it quickly. I was surprised and confused. Al had never come on to me. He had never even made a pass at me. Maybe she'd heard him wrong. Or maybe he did say "Tiffany", but he sure as heck wasn't talking about me.

"Are you sure?"

"Oh yes, I'm sure. Let me tell you something, Tiffany, in case you didn't know, sleeping with someone else's husband can get you killed."

"I'm not sleeping with your husband. If he's sleeping with a Tiffany, it damn sure isn't me. I hope you find her, but you are barking up the wrong tree. Now, would you kindly leave my office? And shut the door behind you," I said to hear and looked down at the papers on my desk.

Boom!

She slammed her hands down on my desk and then she slapped the pen that I was holding out of my hand. She smirked as I stood up. She looked as though she was going to say something else, but once I took a step, she turned around and headed out of my office, slamming the door behind her.

I wanted to chase after her but I forced myself to take my seat. I was a professional, but baby, she was messing with the wrong one! I might make a few millions a year, and sashay around this office in a nice blouse and a skirt, but I was the same girl from around a way, and I didn't mind kicking her ass right out of those overpriced Louis Vuitton's that she was wearing.

I wasn't her husband's mistress. If she didn't believe me, she could ask my under-serviced coochie.

Besides, I didn't have time to worry about someone else's husband. I was too busy trying to find my own. After sending an e-mail to Al, about the incident, I checked my cell phone. I was hoping to see a call from Tobias, but as of yet he hadn't reached out to me.

In my opinion, the somewhat date had been amazing.

Tobias was definitely my type of guy. He was completely different from my ex-husband Ray, but I liked it. And though I had only spent about four hours with him, I liked him. I mean he was charming, funny, and he seemed to have all of his ducks in a row. He didn't seem intimidated when I told him about my position or how much money I made and he even seemed to have that whole dominate, in charge thing going on, which I found very attractive.

Now, I was just waiting for him to call. I'd said all of the right things. I'd given him more than enough hints that I was interested. The bait was set. All he had to do was bite.

I looked up just as my assistant knocked on the door.

"Sorry, to bother you, but the alarm on your car is going off outside. No one was near it when I pulled up but, your windshield has a brick stuck in it. Just so you know."

I didn't even try to be professional as I stormed out of my office and headed towards Al's.

"AL!!!!!"

~***~

"Girl, how did you mess that up?" My sister Shelly asked as she sat across from me drinking a glass of wine. I'd filled her in on my flat tire incident, and my late dinner with Tobias, from a few nights ago. He still hadn't called me and I was confused.

"Does it really matter who calls who first?"

"Uh, hell yeah!"

"What if I text him? It's just a text."

"No Strawberry. If he's interested, he will call you. Maybe you scared him away, with your nasty self. You really asked him to come home with you?"

"I didn't mean to."

"Like hell you didn't. One day you are gonna meet your match," she joked, but I was still thinking about Tobias.

I mean, I thought that we'd hit it off, but maybe he was just being nice. And Shelly was right. Reaching out to him first would make me seem desperate. If he wasn't calling, it was for a reason. Maybe he just wasn't as interested as I'd wanted him to be.

"What did your boss say about his wife? Did she admit to throwing that brick through your windshield?"

"Girl, no. Al forced her to come back to the office and he asked her right in front of me and she denied it. But I know that she did it. Who else would've done it?"

"Damn shame. I would've slapped her."

"Oh, I wanted to. Al also cleared my name and told her that he and I had nothing going on. But he didn't have a choice but to confess that it was some other woman that he'd been seeing on the side and just so happens her name is Tiffany too."

"Scandalous!"

"I know. He doesn't even seem like the cheating type. But then again, they never do."

Shelly shrugged.

"Well, who knows, maybe tonight you'll run into someone else and forget all about Mr. Tobias. Just don't offer him the booty within five minutes of the conversation okay?" Shelly placed down her glass and stood up to fix her dress. I mimicked her actions, and soon after, we headed outside.

It was our younger sisters', April's, birthday, and she'd wanted to celebrate at a club. She'd just turned twenty-two and was in her last year of college, so I'd given her $10,000 to do whatever she wanted to do for her birthday.

I was so proud of her. I thought that maybe she was going to take a trip or something, but she wanted some extravagant club birthday bash. Plenty of drinks, loud music, dancing and V.I.P; and it surprised me. She was so soft spoken, but that was what she wanted. I sure as hell didn't want to be in a club. But in this case, I didn't have a choice. Though I preferred to be at home, catching up on work, or simply doing anything else, since it was her birthday, I agreed to go. But mentally I was already counting down the minutes until I was back at home in my pajamas.

I was in my mid-thirties so the clubbing days, for me, were long gone. I graduated college and jumped right into the work force. Then I met my ex-husband and got married. Soon after that, I got a big promotion, and so I didn't have time to club or have much fun after that. I was always too busy chasing a dollar, and once I caught it, I figured out that I'd lost everything else along the way. Being successful is nothing if you don't have anyone to share your accomplishments with. So, maybe a little fun in my life was just what I needed.

But needless to say, I only lasted for about an hour or so before I told my sisters goodnight. The music was too loud, not to mention, I didn't understand a word that they were saying, and the blinking, colorful lights were making me dizzy. It was time for my old ass to go home.

Heading out of the night club, I didn't realize how far I had to walk to the parking lot to my car. I should've at least asked them to walk me out. After walking for what seemed like forever, I found my car and just as I pressed the unlock button on my keys and opened the door, someone closed it.

"Give me your purse."

Something pressed firmly against the small of my back.

"Wh-what?"

"I said, give me your purse. Now!" The person screamed, splattering spit all over the side of my face. I was being mugged? In this neighborhood?

I glanced side to side, without moving my head, just to see if someone was close by. Being that I didn't see anyone, with shaking hands, I reached the man that was breathing heavily behind me, my clutch.

I tried to recall everything that was in it. My debit card and my license, a few dollars and some gum. I felt the object come off of my back and the next sound I heard was running. I turned around to get a glimpse of the man but he was running full speed down the street.

With my keys still in my hand, I hopped inside of my car and locked the door. Taking long, deep breaths, I tried to calm myself down. For some reason, the incident made me think about my secret. I'd been waiting for years for something to happen to me because of it. I knew that eventually Karma would catch up to me. No matter how hard I tried to stay out of her way. I guess for a second, I thought that maybe this was it, this was the payback for what I'd done; but lucky me, it was only a mugging.

I shook away the thoughts of the horrible thing that I'd done years ago, and thoughts of calling the police entered my mind. I needed to report this or something. My phone started to vibrate from inside of my bra where I'd tucked it while inside of the club.

I thought that it was one of my sisters and I couldn't wait to tell them what had just happened to me but I was wrong. It was Tobias.

Really? After all of this time, why did he have to be calling…like right now?

I stared at the phone. I need to call the police. I need to tell them what had just happened to me. But it had been days and he hadn't called and I couldn't help but wonder why he was calling now. What if he didn't call again?

I was shaken up, but it wasn't like I was hurt or anything. Besides, I knew a policeman, and that would give me a reason to call him and be nosey; not to mention I owed him a good cursing out for the way that he'd screwed me, only to tell me that he was about to get married the next day. My ex-husband Ray was an officer. Well, not just an officer anymore; he was like a chief or lieutenant or something. But it was all the same to me. I was sure that he could tell me what I needed to do about the mugging.

Shaking my head, afraid that the vibration was about to come to an end, I took a deep breath, and finally, I answered the ringing phone.

"Hello?"

"Hello beautiful, sorry to call so late. Are you awake?"

I started up the car and pulled off before responding. I drove like a bat out of hell in the direction of my house. I still felt so uneasy about what had happened to me, but I swallowed my discomfort and answered him.

"Yes."

"I'm sorry I haven't had a chance to call. I had death in the family and had to go out of town. I found out that night after dinner that my grandmother passed away."

"Oh no, I'm so sorry to hear that."

"Thank you. She lived a long, full life, and she was ready to get to that Heaven that she was always talking about. She even appeared to be smiling as she laid in her casket, so I'm sure she made it there safe and sound. But despite everything, you've been on my mind. My plane just landed about two hours ago. I couldn't wait to get settled to give you a call."

"Really?"

"Yes really."

"Why?"

"Why what?"

"Why couldn't you wait to talk to me?"

"Well, it seemed like we hit it off pretty well the other night. Unless it's just me and I misread the signals," he said.

I cleared my throat. My body had stopped shaking and I'd almost forgotten what had happened to me prior to hearing his voice. Almost.

"No. I was actually a little sad that you didn't call. I thought that maybe I'd misread them."

Tobias chuckled. "No. You definitely have my attention Strawberry. I'm a little more than interested perhaps. And not just because you tried to give me the booty as a thank you for changing your tire," he laughed again.

"No. It wasn't like that. I swear."

"Yeah, right, sure it wasn't. So, I'm wide awake. Shall we pick up where we left off? The conversation was getting pretty good if I remember correctly. It was getting juicy. I think you were just about to tell me how freak nasty you are. Now don't be stingy with the details. Talk slowly and don't leave anything out," Tobias chuckled. He definitely had a sense of humor, and I just loved it. He was so down to earth and talking to him just seemed easy. I found it hard to pretend to be something or someone that I wasn't. I was simply being myself with him and it hadn't scared him away.

Pulling into my drive way, I turned my car off, and literally ran inside of the house. Since whoever had my clutch, had access to my address from my license, I turned on the alarm that I hardly ever used.

"Okay," I muffled, trying to catch my breath.

"Okay. So, Strawberry, tell me everything."

We talked for hours and hours until the sun came up. We talked about our childhood. Our parents and siblings. We talked about our past relationships and our first loves. And the sex talk was out of this world! He had me all hot and bothered and from the sound of it, he was that match that Shelly vowed that one day I would meet.

He was perfect.

I woke up to him snoring in my ear. I smiled, decided to let him sleep and hung up the phone. After showering and going outside to get the newspaper, only to find my stolen clutch on the front porch, I called my ex-husband Ray and asked him to stop by.

"I don't know Ray. All I know is that someone came from behind, took my clutch, and then today, I walked outside to find the clutch on the front porch with everything still inside of it."

"And they didn't take anything?"

"No. They didn't even take the cash that I had inside. Why would they mug me for it but not take the cash at least? Why bring it back? And since they did bring it to my house, they obviously looked on my license for my address. That can't be a good thing right? Am I safe?"

"I'm not sure Tiffany. Let me see it and I'll have it checked for finger prints," Ray said. I headed to retrieve my clutch from the bar. I just didn't understand why someone would go through all of that only to return my belongings the next day. It just didn't make sense.

"Here," I reached it to him and as he took it, I glanced at his shiny, new ring.

"So, you really did get married?"

"Yes. About that day…"

"Save it. It's fine. Really. Just let me know if you find anything," I said to him. I was high on "Cloud-Tobias" so I no longer cared about Ray's intentions or his new wife. I was more interested in seeing what might come of whatever this was between Tobias and I.

Ray headed out and Shelly walked in with a giggle.

"Y'all weren't doing "it" again, were you?"

"Nope."

"So, what was he doing here?"

I hadn't told them about the mugging, and at that moment I decided not to. At least not right now. I was fine. Ray was going to check out things for me, and I didn't want them to worry. And with Shelly's big mouth, she would tell everyone, getting them all worked up, even if she promised that she wouldn't.

"None of your business."

"Um huh. So, last night, some random woman came up to me and asked me where you went," she said.

"What do you mean?"

"She tapped me on the shoulder and said "Where did Tiffany go?" I didn't get her name, and to be honest, I barely looked at her face. I just glanced at her, and then I screamed over the music, telling her that you left. She must have known you though. Since she called you by name and all."

I didn't remember seeing anyone I recognized and I was almost positive that none of my colleagues would be in a place like that, but then again, you never know. Maybe it was someone I worked with, especially if they called me Tiffany.

"Anyway, I can't stay long, but about that loan," she said. I headed to my coffee table where I'd left the main purse that I carried, the night before.

"I missed three days last week, and I'm short on daycare. I don't need too much. Just daycare. I don't want it to be too much where Brian would notice. I'll just tell him I made an arrangement with them."

I grabbed my check book. "How much?"

"$600."

"What about $6,000?"

"No Strawberry. Just $600."

I wrote the check and handed it to her.

"I'll pay you back."

"Don't worry about it."

"No. I'll pay you back," she said, kissed my cheek and headed out. I watched her until she backed out of the driveway and headed down the street.

Just before I closed the door, I noticed that her husband Brian had been parked across the street the whole time. He looked at me in a weird kind of way. I waved at him but he simply half-smiled and then headed in the same direction as Shelly.

Was he following her? Weird.

~***~

"You ruined my life...and now, bitch, I'm going to take yours!" the gun sounded and I jumped up, clutching my chest.

Breathe Strawberry. It was just a dream. Just breathe.

I was used to having nightmares. And it was always the same one. Always the exact same thing.

I headed to the kitchen for a cold glass of water. Here lately, I couldn't get my terrible secret off of my mind. Usually I lived life, without even thinking about it, until something brings it back to my mind. The mugging definitely triggered the memory of it.

Years ago, a little while before meeting my ex-husband, I did something terrible.

I was fresh out of college and hurriedly I jumped into the workforce. I was the oldest. Mama needed help with the girls. Daddy was gone so she needed help with bills. I'd worked to put myself through college, along with financial assistance of course, and I graduated at the top of my class. I was eager to make a name for myself.

So, after looking for a few months to no avail, I came up with another strategy. I started putting myself in environments of wealthy business men. And then from there, I used what was in between my legs, just as much as what was in my head for a while and eventually I ended up with a decent job, making decent money.

I'd worked for a company, before the one that I worked for now, for about two years before my current company stole me away. But though I hadn't gotten the position just by what was on my resume, I was really good. I worked hard. I tried to prove myself but no matter what I did, I was overlooked. I was the only African American employee at the company, and had I not shown one of the top executives a really good time, and recorded it, I was sure that I would have never been hired in the first place.

But once I was there, I did my part. I did more than my part, but no one ever seemed to notice. After some time, a top level position came open. I could do the job in my sleep and they knew it too. I deserved that job but because of the color of my skin, and because I was a woman, they brought in someone else. He didn't even have the experience and they hired him because they didn't want to give the job to me. But I wasn't just going to take it. No. I just couldn't take it.

The man that they hired was Jake Dawson. He actually wasn't the one at fault, but he came in with a horrible attitude and treated me like a servant and not like the educated, intelligent, professional woman that I was. He didn't respect me at all; actually said that I was lucky to be there. The disrespect was at an all-time high, but that was nothing little ole' me couldn't fix.

I was angry. So, one day, I seduced him.

I came on to him one night late at the office. I didn't use my hands, just my words, since I knew that the cameras could see but not hear us. I asked him to follow me to my apartment. He did and then I asked him to give it to me rough. He played right into my little trap. I had him choking me. Spanking me and pulling my hair. And once he left, I tore up my house, verified a few marks on my body from the rough four-play that I'd demanded and then I called the police.

I lied and said that he followed me home, and raped me.

Now that I'm older, I know how stupid it was. It was an awful lie. But at the time I was so full of hatred and anger, and I'd let it get the best of me. I felt used. I felt overlooked. I felt mistreated. And I wanted what was mine. I deserved that position. I needed it and they'd just given it to someone else. So I took matters into my own hands.

He had a clean record so worst case scenario, I thought that he would just get a slap on the wrist if it ever went that far. But I never planned for it to. After he was arrested and fired, I planned to simply drop the charges.

He was arrested at work the next morning. He called me a liar and begged me to tell the truth but I didn't say a word. I watched him get handcuffed, and I didn't say a single word. The company was terrified of what legal actions that I might take against them next, so they fired him before they could even get him out of the building and offered me his job.

That was all I'd wanted. The next day, I went to drop the charges. I made up some sad story about my childhood and public shame. I even blamed myself and said that I'd probably made him think that I wanted it and said it was my fault that he misread the signals. I dropped the charges. I told them that I no longer wanted to go through with any of it but...the State picked them back up. They proceeded with the case. They had my testimony, my "rape" kit, pictures of the bruises on my neck and other parts of my body, and so they said that they were continuing with the case.

I watched the public bash him. I watched him and his family be humiliated, and I couldn't do anything about it. And it was all my fault.

I guess he caught the judge on a bad day or maybe she was on her period or something but she had no mercy on him and said that she didn't care that he didn't have any prior troubles. She wanted to make an example out of men of power or of a certain pay rate that thought that they were above the law and she gave him the maximum 10 years in prison.

All because of me. All because of a lie.

I'll never forget the look on his face that day as they led him out of the courtroom. It was more than hatred. I couldn't exactly put it into words. I felt so bad that at that moment I wanted to confess everything but I knew that I couldn't. I knew that I could never tell a soul what really happened. I knew that I could never tell the truth.

I'd tried to fix it but I couldn't. I'd sent an innocent man to prison for a job that I hadn't kept longer than six months afterwards; before LNDC Designs, stole me away. Being that they were back here in California, back near family and friends, and they'd offered me an initial job as Creative Director, that at the time was double what I was making at the company in Chicago, it was the best move for me. So it all had been for nothing.

And just as I was preparing to move, I received the news that that Jake had hung himself in prison. He killed himself and left a note saying four words: I didn't do it.

I was heartbroken as I watched his wife, and his young son on TV. She cried and she told the reporters that she never believed that he did it but that the judge and the whole world did.

And innocent man was dead and his blood was on my hands. Ever since then, I had nightmares and I always had the feeling that someday, someone would come for revenge. It had been over a decade and I hadn't had any problems but I knew that if none of his family ever came to avenge his name, I knew that karma would have her way with me instead.

Heading back to my bedroom, I checked the alarm again, just to make sure that it was on. If I could take it all back I would, but since I couldn't. And one day, I knew that I was going to have hell to pay.

~***~

"Shelly, what about this one?"

She frowned.

"I don't like that one. What about this one?"

I mimicked her previous face expression.

Our style in clothing was completely different. I'd invited her and our little sister on a shopping-date. There was nothing like having a little girl time, with two of my favorite people.

I loved my sisters to death. There was nothing that I wouldn't do for them. I practically helped raised them; especially April. I had been taking care of her for as long as I could remember. She was just like my own daughter. But she was a little different. As I watched her look at clothing, she wasn't saying much. She liked the club scene and she loved to drink, like any other college student, but still, she was different. She always had been.

If she didn't have alcohol in her system, she rarely had much to say. It was as if she was always scared of saying or doing the wrong thing or something. Shelly and I were both outspoken, but she was nothing like us.

"April, you can get anything that you want. No matter the price. It's all on me."

"Okay," was all that she said.

"Oh, you already know that I'm about to rack up," Shelly joked. But she had an arm full of stuff.

Looking past her, I noticed a woman, wearing a pair of sunglasses in the distance. When I looked at her, she looked down as though she was shopping, but I was sure that she had been looking at us.

She didn't look like anyone that I recognized, so I didn't look at her again until we were leaving the store. She still appeared to be shopping, and she smiled at us as we headed out the door. I glanced back just in time to see her put the things that she was holding back on the rack. She didn't buy anything and instead of exiting the same way that we had, she walked towards the other door on the other side of the building.

Hmm...

****

CHAPTER THREE

"Did you borrow that dress from your grandma?"

I gasped and look down at myself.

"I'm just kidding. You looking stunning," Tobias complimented me.

We were going on our first official date, since the first time was a spare of the moment type of thing. We were all dressed up. Though we hadn't planned to match, we did, and as a whole, we looked really good together. Though, I appeared to be a little overdressed.

"So where are we going?"

"To my house."

I looked at him. I don't know what kind of date he thought this was, but if he was gonna try to be nasty, I sure as hell wasn't going to stop him. But he could at least feed me first.

Twenty minutes later, we pulled up at a beautiful, white house. It didn't really seem like his style, but it was gorgeous to say the least. Helping me out of the car, we didn't head for the front door. Instead, he led me to the back yard.

I smiled and Tobias looked at me as though he'd wanted to see my facial expression.

There were lights everywhere. On the ground, dangling from a tent. Everywhere. There was a big plush blanket with about fifty pillows, and an extra blanket, lying neatly on top of it. There were a few bottles of wine, ice, fruit and cheese. There was also two individual baskets and two wine glasses beside each one of them. Rose petals where on the blanket, the ground, all around the pool and even floating inside of it. And there was a big huge screen with and table with some kind of movie projector in front of it.

"This is how I like to do dinner and a movie. I hope you're okay with it."

"I love it," I answered honestly. I told him how beautiful everything was as he helped me out of my shoes.

"None of this is a beautiful as you. But now those feet, that's a different story. Is that a bunion I see on your big toe?" He joked as he made sure that I was comfortable on the blanket.

"Uh no, my feet are perfect," I smiled at him as he took off his shoes and took a seat beside of me. From there we talked and laughed, and enjoyed the subs and salads that he'd prepared inside of the picnic baskets. And then, finally, we got cozy, poured a glass of wine and started the movie.

"I've never had a date like this before. No one has ever taken the time to do something like this for me. Thank you," I said to him. I wanted to kiss him but I didn't know if he wanted to kiss me back.

"You're welcome," was all that he said and squeezed me closer to him. I felt so safe in his arms. I felt good. It felt right. The night went by with a breeze and after we drank about five bottles of wine, laughed, and watched two movies, we ended up falling asleep underneath the stars.

Tonight, instead of nightmares, my dreams were all of him. Part of them were sweet. The others were nasty. I'd forgotten what if felt like to be so in tune with the opposite sex. To feel wanted. To feel complete. I could only pray that he felt the same way.

A cool wind kissed my body and before I could reach for the extra blanket, I felt it as it covered me up. I smiled and just barely opened my eyes, thinking that Tobias had felt the wind too, but I saw feet. Bare feet. And the bottom of a white dress gliding past the pool and soon out of sight.

Who was that?

I tried to open my eyes a little more, but I couldn't. They were just so heavy and seconds later, I drifted back off into a deep, drunken sleep.

"Someone was here last night. A woman. She put blanket on us," I said to Tobias once I'd finished using the bathroom inside of the small pool house.

"Humph. It must have been my maid, Isabelle. She prepared this for us and she must have come back to see how it all went."

I smiled at him as he hugged me.

"Come on. Let me get you home before we are both late for work."

We didn't go inside of his house. Instead, he drove me home, walked me to the door, and then rushed off so that he wouldn't be late. Still on cloud nine, I did the same, and forty-five minutes later, I headed out the front door.

"I came by yesterday evening. You weren't here," Ray said, about to knock, just as I opened the door.

"Whoo! You startled me. And uh, yes. I was um, on a date."

"Oh. There was someone leaving when I pulled up. A White Mercedes?"

White Mercedes?

"Al? My boss is the only one that I know with a car like that. He must've needed me for something. I'd had my phone turned off for most of the night. Maybe he'd called and couldn't get a hold of me. I have to go Ray. Was this about the clutch?"

"No. I just wanted to come by and see how you were doing. You know, since the mugging and everything."

I looked at him strangely.

What was with the sudden interest? A year without saying anything, and all of a sudden, just like that he was back in my life. I couldn't help but think that it was something else to it.

"Are you sure that your new wife would approve of you checking on your old wife?" I asked him as I got into my car. He didn't answer me. He simply smiled, got into his car and drove away and I headed to the office.

"Al did you come by my house last night?"

"No. Why?"

"No reason. I thought I saw your car pulling out of my driveway, as I turned on my street," I lied.

"Oh. Nope. It wasn't me," he said and disappeared.

I wondered who it was then. I didn't know anyone else with a car like that. Maybe they had the wrong address. Or maybe they were just pulling into my driveway to turn around. I do it all the time.

As I got settled at my desk, I beamed at the text messages that were coming through from Tobias.

"You will be mine." One of the messages said and I smiled from the deepest part of my heart. I sure hope so.

I caught a glimpse of Al's wife heading to his office. She looked at me and rolled her eyes. I guess she still didn't believe me, but that was her problem because the way I see it, is that the longer she thought that it was me, the longer this other "Tiffany" would continue to have sex with her husband.

Boom!

~***~

"I'm sorry, I'm using this one," I said.

I was at the gym. Since I was now officially seeing someone, I figured that I could stand to lose a few pounds.

"I said, I'm in here," I said again as someone tried to come into the stall that I was using. They were pulling on the door handle. Didn't they see that it was locked? Looking at the floor, I could see her pink and blue work out shoes as she just stood there.

"I'm using this one," I said again, waiting for her to walk away. But she didn't. She just stood there. I prepared to finish using the bathroom and as I unrolled the tissue, I saw the shoes step away. And then I saw her hand and...

What the hell!

The whole roll of paper towels was on fire!

She had literally lit the roll and threw it underneath the stall door! I jumped to my feet with my pants and panties still down and started to stomp on the blazing roll of paper towels. I flushed the toilet just as the lace on my left shoe started to burn. Once the water in the toilet was clear, I scooped as much water as I could with my hands and started to throw it on the paper towels. It was burning as though it had been dipped in lighter fluid or something. It was taking forever to get the fire completely out. With the flames finally gone, and with my heart beating faster than a speeding bullet, I opened the stall door. Two ladies walked in and looked down at my exposed coochie. I had forgotten to pull up my pants. Immediately, I covered myself and looked at their feet. Neither of them had on the shoes that I'd seen underneath the door

The women stood looking at me as I got myself together.

"Did you see anyone leave out?" I screamed at them for no apparent reason and they both shook their heads no. Pissed off to the max, I stormed out of the bathroom and into the gym. I looked at ever woman's feet that was in sight but as expected, after a stunt like that, whoever she was, was gone.

Oh she was lucky! I would've stomped her into a coma! Grabbing my things, I headed out of the gym madder than a size 16 pair jeans, on a size 20's ass!

I got into my car and just I started to leave, I saw a white Mercedes drive out of the parking lot, similar to my boss Al's car. My mind started to wonder and I started to follow them but as I tried to pull off, my car cut off and the gas symbol popped on.

What? I'd just gotten gas before I came. Frustrated, I found my phone and called Tobias.

"You will not believe what just happened to me!"

~***~

I stared at Jake's wife. The man that had gone to prison and died because of me.

I'd found her on social media. After the incident at the gym and some of the other crazy things that had been going on lately, my gut told me to see what she had been up to.

I looked through her pictures. She was remarried. She looked happy and had two more kids on top of the son that she'd had with Jake. I stared at the boy. He looked just like him. He was smiling and he seemed happy.

They all seemed happy.

I logged off of the computer and sipped my wine in the dark. I was overthinking things. She was happy and she wasn't worried about me.

Sometimes, some things just happen. Yeah, things just happen. I continued to drink my wine, until I heard a sound. I followed it to the front door. The knob was moving. It was turning back and forth. Of course it was locked, but they turned it a few more times and I sat down my glass.

I tip-toed in that direction and once I made it to the door, I looked through the peep hole. No one was there. I moved to the window. I didn't see a car, or anyone, or anything out of the ordinary.

Maybe I've had too much to drink. I stood and stared at the knob for a few seconds and once nothing happened, I headed to bed.

Get it together Strawberry. Get it together.

~***~

"He didn't answer. But he will call me right back. If he doesn't answer, he always calls me right back."

"Uh oh, you know what they say about men who never pick up but always calls you back right?"

"No Shelly, I don't. But I'm sure that you're going to tell me."

"Sure is. They say that they probably have a woman. 90% percent of the time."

"Well, I guess Tobias is in the 10% that don't because I can assure you that he's single."

"And how is that?"

"For starters, I've slept at his house a few times. He never so much as locks his phone. Not that I've tried to go through it or anything. But I noticed that he doesn't lock it. And we talk off and on all day long. If I'm not at his place, or if he isn't at mine, we fall asleep on the phone all night. So, I'm pretty sure that he's single."

Shelly turned up her lips. "Humph. Well, maybe you got lucky then."

"And I didn't say that he never answers. I said if he doesn't, he always calls me right back."

"Oh."

"I really, really like him Shelly. He's so amazing! And funny! Girl, all he does is make me laugh."

"So, when do we get to meet him? Y'all have been talking for a while now."

"Saturday. At the gathering for Mama. And then afterwards, finally, I'm going to show him what he's been missing," I said, licking my index finger with my tongue.

"Eww! Just nasty! So, you haven't slept with him yet?"

"No. I didn't want to seem easy."

"But you are easy."

I hit her with a pillow. "So. But he doesn't need to know that." We both laughed and once my phone started to ring, I held up a finger at her.

"Hello?"

"Hey, you called? My phone was at my desk."

Tobias worked with stocks. And it must pay him pretty well because he had a beautiful house, a nice car, and he had been showering me with dinners and gifts for weeks. He was definitely treating me like a queen. Spoiling me with time as well as with material things that were out of the normal. He'd sent me a painting, and an antique jewel bracelet that was the epitome of beauty. He'd purchased me a "star". Like a real one. Had it registered or something and everything.

I was actually calling him now to thank him for the flower delivery that was waiting for me when I got home on the front porch. I'd told him that I was fascinated with exotic flowers, flowers in general, and for the past two weeks, every day, he sent me a vase full of a different kind. They all came with note cards with special facts about them and even a few came with seeds, if they were capable of being grown in the California climate. My house looked like a damn funeral home, but I loved every bit of it. I was in awe at how thoughtful he was and how attentive he was to everything that I said.

"Thank you for the flowers, again," I chimed.

"No thanks needed. Are you still at the office?"

"No, actually I came home on time today because my sister was dropping by."

"Oh, okay. Well, would you like me to stop by on my way in?"

"Of course. If you're not too tired."

"I'm never too tired to see you."

I blushed. He gave me butterflies.

"Do you want me to cook tonight or will you be grabbing something?"

"If you're going to cook, I'll eat whatever you make. I'm still trying to figure out if it's your cooking that's been giving me diarrhea though. I'm not saying that it's your food but what I am saying is that it didn't start until you started offering to cook for me, so...I mean maybe..."
Tobias was laughing and I wished that he was in front of me so that I could give him the finger.

"Shut up. I'll fix you some food." After a few more words, we said our goodbyes.

"Um, he got you cooking and shit. And you ain't even tested or tasted the "meat" yet. Must be nice," Shelly laughed as my phone rang again.

It was Tobias again, so I answered.

"Hello?"

Tobias was talking but not to me.

"Hello? Hello?"

I pressed the phone up against my ear. He was screaming. Or maybe even in an argument or something. I wasn't sure. I'd never so much as heard him raise his voice before so it kind of threw me for a loop.

"But why did you do it! What was the point? You do your job. I'll do mine. I don't need you to do my damn job!" He screamed. Well, he was the manager, and apparently he was coming down hard on one of his employees. And he'd cursed. I cursed at times on the job, but I kept it at a minimum. He had better be careful with that.

The yelling continued and figuring that he must have accidentally called me, I hung up.

Shrugging my shoulders, I smiled at Shelly. "Come on. Let's go see what I have in here to cook. By the way, I forgot to tell you that Brian followed you here that day."

"What?"

"The day that you borrowed the money for daycare, I saw him. He was parked across the street."

Shelly looked concerned. "Funny, he didn't mention it."

I wanted to offer her money again, but I knew that she was going to decline it, so I dropped the subject. Remembering Brian's face, he looked like a man under a lot of stress and Shelly knew her husband a lot better than I did, so she must be doing the right thing with trying to keep me and my funds out of it.

Shelly stayed for a while longer and then headed home to cook for her own family. Although I was tired, for the next hour and a half I cooked for Tobias but as it turns out, it had all been for nothing because unfortunately, Tobias never came.

~***~

"Knock knock," I smiled at the sight of him. Of course Tobias explained his reasoning for not showing up the other night. He'd had some kind of work disaster, where a lot of money had been charged to the wrong client. I guess that was why he'd been fussing and screaming like a mad man. He'd explained that he had to sort it out before leaving and by the time he'd returned my call around ten that night, I'd already fallen asleep.

"How did you get in here?" I asked him. I was working late at the office since I had a three-day weekend. I had taken Friday off to help prepare for Mama's big party.

My mother, Lola Jay, was turning seventy and we'd decided to throw her a party this year. She made seventy look like forty, so this year we wanted her to feel as young as she looked. We were having a big bash with family and friends, food, music and it was the 70's themed. Hence the idea connection.

"I got lucky. Some worker was on the way out and I told her that I was an employee and running up to my office. She was on the phone and I told her that I'd forgot my badge and she let me right on in. But I knew that if I wanted you out of here, I was going to have to come and drag you out of here myself," Tobias smiled and walked towards me.

I looked at him from top to bottom. He was just so damn sexy. From the way that he dressed to the way that he stood up against the door. Everything about him just drove me wild.

"So, I got a question for you," he said.

"What?"

"What color panties do you have on?" he asked with a grin.

"Well, is bare-ass considered a color? I'm not wearing any panties today," I flirted with him. I could tell that he wasn't expecting my response and that he was trying to figure out if I was serious or not. But he made the first attempt to find out.

Tobias made his way over to me and slid his big, strong hands underneath my skirt and smiled.

"You are so nasty…but I like it," he growled, standing me up and without warning, he picked me up off of my feet.

"What are you doing?"

"Who me? Oh nothing. Just working late," he said as he started to kiss my neck.

Of course I was the only one left at the office, so we were all alone. I'd planned to make things special for him this weekend, but office sex just seemed so much better. I was as excited as a prostitute in a car full of tricks. I'd been trying to play the "get to know you" role, but I had long since been ready for some action. And finally, I was about to get some.

I felt my skirt rise over my butt and then he sat me on the edge of my desk.

"Can you do one thing for me?" I was in a daze as he kissed my neck but I nodded my head anyway.

"Whatever you do...DON'T tell me to stop," and once he finished his sentence, he laid me on top of the piles of papers and opened my legs.

For some reason I felt just a little scared.

What in the hell was then man about to do to me?

I mean, duh, I knew the obvious answer, but the look in his eyes told me that he was about to put something on me that might not be able to shake off. I didn't need anything that was going to make me crazy or have me sitting outside his house.

But as he licked his lips, I already knew that he was about to get down to business.

And I was right. No words were spoken. No warning was given as he placed his mouth on me. The things that he did with his tongue made me want to punch him in the back of the head. I balled my fists up and everything, twice, I swear I did.

For a moment I had to check to make sure that I was still breathing because it seemed as though his mission was to suck out my soul through my vagina. The more he slurped, the more I moaned. My body was shaking as though it was going through withdrawals. My hips tried to battle with his tongue, but I lost as he locked my legs into position and worked his tongue like a merry-go-round. I disobeyed him and begged him to stop, over and over again. But he didn't listen; and I was glad, because I hadn't meant it.

I allowed him to continue exploring my deepest domain and then it was my turn. And I showed him how it was done. He howled to the moon and for what seemed like hours, we satisfied each other in every way possible. As he wrapped my legs around his waist, I looked into his eyes and they said exactly what I wanted them to say.

He was now mine. And I was now his.

And I didn't have a problem with that.

~***~

"Tiffany Parks? What's your pin number?"

I pressed my phone up against my ear.

"Excuse me?"

"This is IMCD Security. What is you pin number?"

"4147"

"Now that you are verified, we are calling to inform you that there is an intruder in your home. The alarm was set off because the back door has been kicked in. Police are in route."

My heart dropped and I hung up the phone. We were out getting a few last minute items for the party, but I hurriedly grabbed Tobias's hand and ran out of the store. I explained what was going on as I drove and by the time that we got to my place, the police were already there.

"Hi, this is my house," I said, rushing past them. They asked me to look around. Nothing seemed to be missing. Honestly, it didn't look as though they'd touched anything at all.

"The alarm must have scared them off. The dirty footprints show that they came in for just a second, only in here and in there, but they were gone before we got here. Any ideas who would have done this?"

I shook my head no. After a few more minutes, we talked and then the police took off.

First a mugging. And now a break-in.

Was somebody trying to get my attention?

Tobias headed to the back door to see what he needed to do to fix it.

"I'll go get some clothes and stay here with you for a while, if that's okay. No pressure, I just can't have you staying here alone."

"I would like that. I would feel safe if you were here with me." I would feel safer if he'd said that I could come stay with him at his house, but since he hadn't suggested it, I would take what he was offering.

Tobias continued to inspect the door and this dreadful feeling seemed to surround me all at once.

Something wasn't right. I could feel it.

Something just wasn't right.

****

CHAPTER FOUR

I walked into work with a smile on my face. After the little incident at my house, the rest of my weekend was incredible!

Mama's birthday bash was a blast! She had so much fun, and it was so good to see her having the time of her life. And I introduced Tobias to her and the rest of my family.

They loved him! Though we hadn't put a title or label on our relationship, we both knew how much we meant to each other, and with him now staying at my place, until I felt safe enough to stay there alone, we were definitely settling into the role of being a full-blown couple. And I could definitely get used to that; and the penis two or three times a day!

"Tiffany, can I see you in my office, please?"

I looked up at my boss Al and nodded my head.

I'd been working for him for years, and I guess he could also be considered a friend. I mean, kind of. He was very private, and my life until now, had been pretty boring, so I guess we never had a whole lot to talk about; unless it was work. He and I both knew that I made this place run smoothly so that he could sit back and do nothing.

My salary was good, but one day I'd always hoped to take his spot. Hell, he didn't do any work anyway. And since the whole spat with his wife, he has been very distant.

"Have a seat."

I sat down and crossed my legs.

Al turned his laptop around to face me.

"So, tell me why this was in my e-mail this morning," he said.

I looked at the laptop and covered my mouth.

Someone had recorded Tobias and I getting down on my office desk. From the recording, it looked as though they were recording through the window.

"Uh, sir, I can explain."

"Oh can you? Because it looks like you're having sex on your desk. But if there is another explanation, sure, let me hear it."

"I, I, I thought that we were alone."

"Looks like you thought wrong."

"Who sent you the e-mail?"

"It doesn't matter. But you weren't the only one working late that night, for once. Now. I don't have to tell you how bad this is. I don't have to tell you that this is grounds for termination. It's disgusting. Tacky and tasteless."

"Sir. I know. But please don't fire me. Please. I love my job. We've been working together for years."

Al stood up and adjusted his tie. He headed to shut his office door and he closed his blinds.

"You deserve to be fired Tiffany."

"I know sir. But I swear, it will never happen again."

I was already calculating my savings in my head. I could probably live off of it for a long while. I could still maintain all of Mama's bills and mine and I could also finish paying for April's last year of college.

But whether my savings lasted for two, three or five years, at some point, I would need to go back to work.

And who would hire me once they verified my last employment with Al only for him to tell them that I was fired for having sex on the job?

And after all of my years of hard work and long hours in this place, I would just die if he fired me. This job was everything to me. For years, it's been my life. I was good at it. This company needed me. And I needed it.

"Al, it will never happen again."

"Well, maybe just one more time."

I looked at him confused.

"Let me taste it."

"Excuse me?" I couldn't believe my ears.

"You heard me. I've had a thing for you for years. My wife was right. I was fantasying that she was you that night. I want you. I always have. But I'll settle for just a taste of it. The video disappears, you get to keep your job. None of this ever happened. If you just let me taste it," he said as he licked his lips.

I tried to close my mouth but I couldn't.

"I watch you sometimes. Most nights, I make sure that you get home safely. Other nights, I ride by your house just to see if you're there. But that one night that you asked if I'd come by, I swear I didn't. I was at home with her, wishing that I was with you. I don't want her. I want you. But I always played it cool. But since this little opportunity has presented itself, I'm telling you that I want you. I want you bad. So, how bad do you want to keep your job?" Al said.

This fool is what the old folks called, plum crazy! And did he just admit to semi-stalking me?

"One taste. The video goes away."

Taste this sexual harassment lawsuit I'm about to slap on your ass! The one time that I'd left my phone at my desk, I actually needed it. I would've recorded his ass and instead of begging for my job, I would be taking his.

All of this time he's wanted to screw me?

I just couldn't believe it.

His wife crossed my mind. She was right. He had been talking about me. I was sure that he'd lied and told her that he was seeing a "Tiffany" on the side to cover-up his infatuation. It was all a lie.

What was I supposed to do?

If I told him to shove it, let him fire me and then try to go at him with a sexual harassment case, I wouldn't have any proof. I was sure that he would deny it and simply show the video and say that I was just angry about losing my job.

But he was married. Back in the day, I wouldn't have cared, but I was older. I was a grown woman with morals, and standards, and married men belonged to their wives. To me, men wearing a wedding band came with a warning sign: Sluts, this means that he's taken. Keep your hands off!

So what was I supposed to do?

And not only was he married, oh no, he was married with a crazy ass wife. And after hearing that he had been riding by my house, watching me, for only the Man above knows how long, he was crazy too. And screwing a crazy person, with the stuff that I had in between these thighs, just wasn't a good move. He would be stalking me for real.

But then again, he only asked for a taste.

Nothing good would come from this. Maybe firing me was the best option. At least I could walk away with my dignity and my pride. But what good was pride without a paycheck? My decade long career seemed to be flashing before my eyes.

"I'm not asking you for sex. I just want to put my mouth on it. That's it. You can delete the e-mail and video yourself. It'll be our little secret."

I stared into his eyes. He stared back. I knew that he was serious, and I also knew that if I did what he wanted me to do, I knew that he was going to keep his word, and let me keep my job.

Ugh! I couldn't believe that this was happening. I couldn't believe that of all things, this was what he wanted. Thoughts of Tobias tried to attack me, but I fought them off. I had to do what was best for me. Even if I didn't want to.

I took a deep breath, glanced at his locked door and I stood up. He watched me, eagerly, as I lifted up my skirt with shame and pulled down my panties. The sooner we get started, that sooner it would all be over with.

After all, what other choice did I have?

~***~

"Hello?"

"Hello," she said.

"Who is this?"

"Who is this?"

"You called me."

"I know."

"How can I help you."

"You can't."

I looked at the phone. The number was unavailable but I knew that whoever it was, they were trying to change their voice. It sounded like they were holding their nose.

"Shelly, stop playing!"

"Who is Shelly?"

She giggled and then she hung up. I called Shelly.

"Stop playing on my phone chick."

"What? I wasn't playing on your phone," she sounded like she was lying. She let out a small laugh.

"Whatever. I know it was you."

"No it wasn't."

"Anyway, what are you doing?"

"Nothing. Waiting on Brian so I can see how his interview went."

"Did he get the job?"

"I don't know. I hope so."

Shelly's husband Brian was a computer genius. He could do anything with computers, hacking, or IT related and he was as smart as a whip. The last company that he worked for moved their entire company to China, so he'd been looking for new employment ever since.

"Well, call me later. Ray is beeping in."

"Ray?" She asked but I clicked over. But before I could say Hello, he hung up.

Tobias came walking into the living room, wearing nothing but a towel. I bit my bottom lip but the doorbell rung and I put my thoughts on stand-by.

"Sorry. My phone went dead. We got a partial print off of the clutch. As soon as we get a ping on the print, I'll let you know," Ray reached me the clutch. I followed his eyes to what he was looking at behind me.

Tobias.

He was standing with his back towards the door, only wearing a towel and Ray looked disturbed.

"Thank you. I'll talk to you later."

I slowly shut the door in his face and went back to entertaining Tobias.

"What was that about?"

"Oh, well, to be honest, he's my ex-husband. He's remarried now. But I had him checking into something for me."

Tobias didn't look threatened. He simply nodded.

"So, what is this? Is this going anywhere between us? Is this just sex? Fun?"

Tobias dropped the towel and came closer to me.

"This is whatever you want it to be. Hell, I'm falling in love with you. I don't want nobody but you, baby."

Yes! That's just what I wanted to hear!

We started to kiss but we were soon interrupted by a ringing phone.

I glanced at my phone. It wasn't mine.

I glanced at his phone on the coffee table. It wasn't his. What?

I followed the noise to his pants pocket. The ringing stopped, and then started again.

He has another cell phone? Why would he have two phones? We'd been dealing with each other for months now and never had I saw him with another cell phone.

He pouted and headed to answer it.

"Hello?"

He listened and said a few words and then said that he was on his way.

"I'm sorry, I have to go. They need me at the office."

"You have two phones?"

"Yes. It's my work phone. They gave them out to all of the managers the other day. I need to go get dressed," he said, lying the phone beside his other phone on the table.

As soon as he was out of sight, I picked it up.

It was locked.

Why would his work phone have a lock on it, yet he didn't even bother to put a lock on his personal one?

I sat the phones back down and headed in his direction.

~****~

"Now, where did he go?"

I'd let Tobias talk me into going to the flea market, and somehow he always seemed to get away from me. I looked from left to right. I took a few steps and then I spotted the back of his shirt. He appeared to be talking to someone. I was able to see that his mouth was moving as he turned his head side to side, as though he was looking for me but I couldn't see past him to see who he was talking to.

"Hey, looking for me?" I tapped him on the back. He turned around with a smile. I looked past him but no one was there. People were around but there was no one close enough to him that he could have been talking to.

"Come on baby, let's go."

We walked and walked and his phone, the work one, was vibrating like crazy. But Tobias didn't answer it.

"It could be important."

"Being here with you is important. We need some quality time together. They are just going to have to wait."

I kissed him and after another hour or so, finally we were on the way home.

"I'll get all of the bags. Go open the door, Tobias said. I got out of the car and headed in. Leaving the door cracked, I headed to use the bathroom and to change my clothes. Minutes later, I headed to the living room to see that Tobias still hadn't made it in.

I walked outside to see that he was still sitting in the car, in the AC, with the windows up.

I knocked on the window.

He was on the phone and he acted as though he didn't see me. I tapped the window again, but still he didn't look in my direction. I folded my arms and all of two minutes later, finally, he looked at me, moved his mouth for about three more seconds, and then pulled the phone away from his ear.

"Yes dear," he said, opening the door.

"Don't yes dear me. You ignored me."

"It was an important call. You've had me all day and you have me all to yourself for the rest of the night. No phone. No interruptions."

I was still pouting as he kissed my lips and started to get the bags. I followed him with my arms still folded over my chest towards the house and just as I was about to shut the front door, the white Mercedes, road by slowly, and though the windows were tented, I knew who exactly who it was this time by the license plate.

Al.

~***~

"When will you be back?"

"In just a few days. The conference is three days long. They wanted us to fly in today so that we have the whole weekend to prepare." Tobias said as the taxi waited to take him to the airport.

"So what, five days? What am I supposed to do until then? I miss you already," I whined.

"Oh, don't worry. I have a few things that I'm gonna have you do later once I'm settled at the hotel. I didn't buy that whipped cream and chocolate syrup last night for nothing. Watch what I have you doing to yourself later," Tobias warned. Oh. He was so nasty. Just like me.

"Are you sure you are going to be safe? If not, I'll stay."

"I'll be fine. I'll be waiting for you to get back. Love you," I said and as soon as the words came out of my mouth, I noticed that it was the first time that I'd said them. Neither of us had uttered the words, though the feelings were definitely there. He'd said that he was falling in love, but he'd never said the words.

"I love you too," he grinned, kissed me, and got into the taxi and drove away.

Aww!

Yes! He loves me too and I could honestly say that I could feel it. The butterflies in my stomach fluttered around for a little while as the taxi disappeared.

I headed towards the mailbox to check the mail. It was Saturday, and I figured that I could get out and stay gone most of the day and then I was going to call Ray to ask if he could ask a few favors from his police friends to ride by my house, until Tobias got back. Just to be on the safe side.

I looked at the mail and just as I turned to walk up the driveway, I heard my name.

"Tiffany?"

I turned around. Al.

What was he doing here? Though I'd seen him ride by a few days ago, I hadn't mentioned it to him. Ever since the day that I'd let him taste it, things had been so strange. I stayed out of his way and he stayed out of mine and we mostly only communicated via e-mail unless it was at a meeting. I just felt disgusting around him now, and every time that I was in his presence I couldn't help but think of how bad the experience was with him.

He'd licked my pussy like he was a cow. Sloppy and messy. And he snorted in between licks. Worst two minutes of my life!

"What are you doing here?"

"I was just riding by."

The way that he said it creeped me out and when he parked his car, something told me that I should probably start running. So I did.

"You shouldn't be here Al."

"Tiffany. I just want to talk to you. Can I come in?"

He asked, opening his car door and I ran full speed inside of my house and locked the door behind me.

"Tiffany?" he rang the doorbell. And then he rung it again. And then again. And then again. Over and over and over!

"Tiffany! Tiffany! Tiffany! Please let me in!"

He has officially lost it! I'm calling the police!

I grabbed my phone and then suddenly, the ringing stopped. I opened the blinds to see that his wife was now outside of my house, holding a baseball bat.

She must have followed him there. I hoped that she didn't think that he'd been invited. I didn't have a damn thing to do with him showing up, acting like a crazy person. But I was sure that she wouldn't see it that way. They appeared to be arguing and then she swung the bat at him. She missed him the first time, but she damn sure clocked him the next time around. He finally got away from her, got into his car and drove away with her speeding behind him.

I took a deep breath. I wanted to call Tobias, but I didn't want him to worry. He'd already sacrificed enough by staying over at my place, and I didn't want him to be concerned and miss the conference because of me. He loved his job, just as much as I did. So instead of calling him, I called my ex-husband to see if he could get a patrol car to ride by every now and then.

"I'm surprised that you called."

"Well, we are divorced you know. We went over year without talking. Remember?"

"I know, I just…anyway, what's up?"

83

"I need to ask a favor. I'll be staying alone for a few days for the first time in a little while and with the mugging, and the intruder---"

"Intruder?"

"It's a long story. Anyway, could you have someone ride by every now and then just to make sure nothing strange is going on out there that I can't see? Or could you do it whenever you have a few minutes to spare?"

Ray was quiet. I still couldn't exactly say if we were really trying to give this friendship thing a try, or if I was just using him because of his police experience and connections. Either way, at the moment he was a good person to be on my team.

"If you can't, I understand."

"I'll see," he said and then told me that he had to go.

He was trying to be tough but I knew that meant "yes".

I looked outside just to make sure that no one was there and then I grabbed my purse and headed out. I wanted to be away from my house as much as possible. And my biggest concern was that now, I really was going to have to find another job. There was no way that I could keep working there. There was no way that I could be around Al. He had completely lost his marbles. And though it was killing me to even think about it, I was going to have to resign. I guess letting him put his mouth on me had all been for nothing. After today, I just couldn't stay there. I couldn't be around him. And Monday morning, I was going in to get my things, and give him a formal letter of resignation.

I had plenty of savings. Resigning looked better than getting fired. Then I could tell the new employer that I left because my boss had a sexual attraction towards me. But I would take few months off. Hell, now that I was all in love, maybe even a year. Maybe do some things that I'd always wanted to do. For the past thirteen years I'd been working non-stop and though my bank account was lovely, it was time for a change. I hadn't been on a vacation in years. I've taken time from work, but I would go anywhere. Most of the time I would just end up working from home anyway.

I couldn't believe what I was thinking, by my mind was made up. It was my heart that still needed a little convincing.

For the rest of the day, I visited everyone that I could. I even went to check on my little sister and Mama. Since she lived not too far for Tobias's house, I had the idea of just swinging by.

I hadn't been to his house in a long while, since he was staying over at mine. He had so many clothes there now, that he barely ever had to go home to get more. It was as though he had moved in, without realizing it.

Pulling up at his house, it seemed as though every light in the house was on.

Was his maid there?

I knew that he'd said that she wasn't a live in maid, but that she had a key. But he hadn't been there in ages, so what in the world was there to clean?

I didn't see a car parked outside of the garage, and if there were any parked inside of it, I couldn't see those either.

He'd offered to get me a copy of his house key, once, but I'd said that I didn't need it. But at that moment, I wished that I had it.

I decided to get out of the car. I looked in his mailbox. It was empty so I headed to the front porch. Before I could even get all the way to the door I heard music. It was old school music; the kind that made you either want to bust a move or bust a nut. A little rough explanation, but it was the truth. It was that music that made you feel good. It definitely wasn't the kind of music that Tobias liked. He liked old school rap, new school rap, gospel rap; it really didn't matter as long as it was rap.

I pressed my ear up against the door and then I knocked. After knocking again, and because no one answered, I rang the doorbell. Still, no one came to the door.

Hmm…

I stepped back and then I finally walked away. Once in the car, I stared at the house. All of the lights upstairs was on and everything. I was sure that he hadn't left them that way. I checked my phone. I had two missed calls from Tobias. I'd been waiting on his call for hours, and the few seconds I'd stepped away from my phone, he called. I called him back twice, but it was going straight to his voicemail. He must've been trying to call me again.

Cranking up my car, slowly I started to pull off as my phone started to ring. Tobias.

I answered it and glanced back at his house one last time.

Wait.

I just barely caught a glance a someone letting go of the blinds that they had been peeking out of.

Hmmm…

~***~

I walked into work, with my resignation letter in hand. Immediately I could tell that something was wrong.

As I walked by, everyone looked at me and whispered. Entering my office, the head honcho of the company was there, along with a few other top dogs and the police.

"Tiffany? Tiffany Parks?" I nodded.

"We would like to ask you a few questions about your relationship with Al Sherman."

"Relationship? He was my boss."

"Well, his wife says otherwise. She says that it was more than that. She shot him this morning. He's dead. she's going for temporary insanity. And she has a therapist and friends that said they had wondered when something like this was going to happen. Due to tons of emotional stress from his extramarital affairs. She said that you were one of them."

"No. I wasn't."

"So you and Al Sherman never had a sexual relationship?"

"No." I wondered if I should have told them about the oral thing between us in order to keep my job, but there was no way that they could prove it ever happened so I didn't mention it.

"Why would she assume that something was going on between you two?"

"She said that he'd called out my name, "Tiffany", during sex, but I'm not the only woman named Tiffany as I'm sure you know. Maybe he was sleeping with a Tiffany…but not me."

"Did she catch him at your house over the weekend?"

"Yes. He'd tried to get inside of my home."

"Why didn't you let him in? If it was nothing sexual, what were you afraid of?"

"He was acting strange. He scared me. So I ran into the house and locked the door. I wasn't sure why he was at my home or how his wife knew where I lived, but I didn't want to be in the mix of something that I didn't have anything to do with."

"Did you report this incident?"

"Well, I mentioned it to a friend on the force." I really did, but I could fill Ray in later.

"Name?"

"Ray Parks?"

"Parks? Husband?"

"Ex-husband. I kept my last name after the divorce."

"Hmm. Were you aware that your boss, Al, had a video on his computer of you and gentleman having a sexual encounter in what looked like this office?"

What? He'd kept a copy of the video?

I'd personally deleted the e-mail. He must have sent it to another one before mentioning it to me.

"No. I was not aware of that."

"His wife caught him watching it and masturbating to it. That's what pushed her over the edge. Does the gentleman in the video work here?"

"No."

"Name?"

"No. I don't see how that's relevant. Look, I'm sorry about what happened but Al and I had nothing going on. If he had some kind of sick infatuation with me, I have nothing to do with that. I'd come to work to resign today after the incident. I didn't want to work for somebody like that," I said showing him my resignation letter.

"Somebody like what?"

"Like that. Coming to my house, beating on my door, begging me to let him inside."

The cop wrote down a few things and then looked back at me.

"Thank you for your time," he said and made his exit.

"Thank you for your resignation. That will save your face in all of this. I want your things out of here by the end of the day," one of the owners of the company said.

What? What if I'd wanted to change my mind?

But after all of this, I didn't.

I sat back in my chair.

Al was dead?

This was just one big mess. I didn't know exactly how to feel until I opened my lap top and saw e-mail in my inbox titled: HOMEWRECKER. I didn't recognize the email address, and once I opened the email, all it said was: Homewrecker.

I was not a homewrecker! I slammed the laptop shut. Hell, I didn't need it anymore anyway. Placing my head in my hands, I realized that I just needed to breathe. Everything was okay, I just needed to breathe. None of this was my fault. Al's death wasn't my fault.

Grabbing my phone, I called Tobias. He didn't answer.

I called Shelly. She didn't answer either.

So I did something that I hadn't done in years.

I cried.

"Looks like you had a bad day," a woman said, sitting beside me. I was at a karaoke lounge, drinking and listening to some drunk woman, cry to the moon.

I'd had such a long day. I didn't want to go home, because Tobias wasn't there. He wouldn't be home until Wednesday. He'd tried to comfort me over the phone and tell me that everything was going to be okay, but his words hadn't worked. I still felt some kind of way.

Al was dead. And though it wasn't my fault, I felt bad about it. He hadn't deserved to die. I'd gone from a lonely, boring life, to one that seemed to have something going on, every other day.

I'd take my old life back for 200 Alex! As long as I could keep Tobias.

I reached my limit, and then I headed out. Sitting in my car, I didn't want to be alone. I called Shelly, but her husband Brian said that she was asleep. I thought about going to sleep at Mama's or at my little sister April's apartment, but they lived too far for me to drive and I had been drinking.

I had a few friends, but they were all married. The only person that was left was Ray.

I dialed his number. Maybe he could just come and sit with me until I fall asleep.

"Hello?"

I looked at the phone.

"I'm sorry, I was calling for Ray."

"He's asleep. Can I take a message?"

This must be his new wife. I didn't want to cause any problems. Hell, I didn't want his wife to end up killing him too.

"Uh, no, I was just calling to check on something. He was checking into something for me, and I was just calling to see if he had found anything new."

"Okay Tiffany, I'll tell him that you called."

"You know who I am?"

"Of course. How could I not? He has compared me to you since the day that we met."

I didn't like her tone, so I figured that it was best for me to hang up.

"Okay, thank you," I said and I hung up the phone.

Driving off, I tried to focus on the road as I made it to *Walmart's* parking lot. They were open for 24-hours, so I parked as far away from the building as possible, locked my car doors and put my chair back.

I wasn't going home alone, so I closed my eyes, and soon, I fell asleep.

****

Chapter Five

"I don't feel so good."

"It's just stress. Everything is going to be okay,"
Tobias rubbed my back.

Now, it had been a few weeks since Al was killed by
his wife, and since I had resigned from my job. I felt good
about my decision. I'd been sleeping in. Staying up late.
Watching TV, cooking and painting. I loved to paint. I just
never used to have the time to do it. Everything had been
okay, but for the last week or so, I just haven't felt like
myself.

"I don't feel stressed. I just feel weak."

Tobias's phone rung and he held up a finger.

I hate that damn phone!

I guess now that I wasn't working, I was seeing how
busy Tobias really was. His phone, the work one, rung non-
stop, even when he wasn't at work.

He could barely use the bathroom in peace without it
ringing and most evenings, he just turned it completely off.

"Sorry, now what were you saying?"

"Nothing. Are you still going to be able to take a
vacation from work in a few weeks?"

"Anything for you baby. I can't wait to get away with you."

He always knew just what to say. I was so in love with him that it was sickening. I wanted to be around him all the time. When he wasn't around me, all I did was think of him. He was so good to me. If I had a problem with something, immediately, he fixed it. I didn't like something, he changed it. I mean, where did this man come from? He never made me question our relationship. Though I questioned other things.

Like who had been at his house while he was away at the conference?

I told him about it and I assured him that someone had been in there. He'd said that he would ask the maid, but also said that if I'd had a key, like he'd suggested, I could have gone in to make sure everything was okay.

Needless to say, he got me a key made to his house that same day.

"I want you in my life forever," Tobias said, interrupting my thoughts.

"Don't say things that you don't mean. I just might be crazy enough to believe you."

"I mean it. I love you, with your fine ass. And I don't want anyone else to have you," he smiled.

I raised my head to kiss him but it felt extremely heavy so I frowned and he noticed.

"Let me check my bag. I have some pills that were prescribed a while ago for migraines and body aches. They work and they will help you sleep," Tobias said and disappeared out of the room. He came back with a pill and a glass of water. After I took it, he turned off the lights.

Tobias got under the covers and scooted close to me. He wrapped his arms around me and held me close to him. I felt so safe. I felt so loved. These last few months with him, felt like years. I felt as though I'd known him my whole life. I felt so connected to him. I felt so special.

After lying in silence for a while at some point I must have dozed off. I woke up hours later, leaping out of bed, running to the bathroom. Holding my stomach, I threw-up non-stop for all of three minutes.

"Tobias! Tobias!"

I didn't get a response.

Finally, able to pull myself away from the toilet, I glanced back into the bedroom. Tobias wasn't there. Slowly, I walked to the front of the house. He wasn't there either.

Where is he?

I glanced outside. His car was still parked in the driveway, so I walked all over the house. I even checked the backyard, but he was nowhere in sight.

Maybe he went for a late night run or something, but the front door was locked.

I headed back into my bedroom. I found my phone to call him. Looking at the clock, it was 3 a.m. in the morning. Where could he be?

I followed the vibrating noise to the dresser. He'd left his phone. Both of them. Feeling nauseous again, I ran back to the bathroom and after a few more sessions of vomiting, I ended up falling asleep on the floor.

Hours after that, I heard my morning alarm chiming from my phone and I opened my eyes. Once on my feet, I headed to the bedroom and stared at Tobias. He was fast asleep.

"Tobias?"

He groaned and turned over.

"Where did you go last night?"

"What?" he mumbled.

"Where did you go?"

"Nowhere. I didn't go anywhere last night. What are you talking about Strawberry? Good morning baby."

"I woke up last night and you weren't here. I called you but you left your phone."

"What? What are you talking about?" he managed to say just before snoring again.

I headed to my phone to turn off the alarm. I unlocked my phone and checked my call log.

What? I know that I called him. But looking at my call log, I didn't have any record of calling Tobias at 3 a.m. that morning.

I picked up his phone from the dresser. He didn't have a missed call from me either.

I looked at him as he snored. If I hadn't called him, maybe I had been dreaming or something. Wow. Maybe he was right. Maybe I was stressed and bugging out.

But before I could think about it more in depth, I went running to the bathroom…again.

~***~

"You're what?"

"Well, I was surprised too."

"How?"

"Remember that night we went to the movies? That quickie in the bathroom stall? It had to be that night. That was the only time we didn't use protection. You always make sure that we have protection, but you didn't have anything that night. Remember?"

"But I pulled out," Tobias sat down and appeared to be in deep thought.

Yep. I was pregnant.

It was a surprise to me too and I wasn't quite sure as to how I felt about it, but seeing Tobias's reaction, I wasn't sure that it was good news. I mean, we were still getting to know each other. Our relationship, our love, was still new.

I still couldn't believe it. I was thirty-five and I haven't been pregnant since my early twenties. I'd always wanted kids, but years ago, I maybe the assumption that after those two abortions that I had, that I probably couldn't have them. I never got pregnant by Ray; not even once.

So I was shocked.

"I know we haven't been together long. You have a thriving career and well in a year or two, I'll be headed back to work. But it seems to have come at the right time. I'd worked hard all my life and when I decided to take a break and just live, I come up pregnant. I didn't exactly want a baby until marriage, so I don't know what to think or how to feel about this. I don't know if I want it. Do you?" Tobias just sat there.

"Could you say something please?"

He looked at me. "I'm just trying to process this. Okay, just let me process it."

Tobias didn't have any kids and had never been married. He too stated that he only wanted to have them with his wife and when the time was right. But I was six weeks pregnant, and I guess I just expected him to be happy about the news for some reason.

But from the looks of it, he wasn't.

Tobias stood up and came around the table to kiss me. We'd met for lunch like we had been for a while lately.

"I guess we can talk more about it when I get home later," he said and even touched my stomach. With that, he walked away and didn't bother to look back.

~***~

The gun sounded and I jumped up.

"Strawberry, what's wrong?" Tobias sat up beside of me.

"Nothing. Just another bad dream."

Tobias laid down and so did I. He pulled the covers over me and I stared at the window.

I smiled at the small streaks from the moonlight that peeked through the blinds. In a strange way, looking at it relaxed me. Just as I was about to close my eyes, a shadow moved and caught my attention.

I stared at the window. The shadow moved again and I even heard sticks on the ground break underneath their feet.

There is definitely someone out there. I stared at the shadow. It was as if they knew that I was awake. I waited for them to move again, but they didn't. The shadow was still. I nudged Tobias, who had started back snoring.

"Tobias. Tobias," I whispered and nudged him again.

I looked back at him.

"Tobias."

"What?" he mumbled. I looked back at the window. The shadow was gone. I waited to see if I saw any movement. I listened to see if I heard anything. But everything was quiet. Everything was still.

"What?" Tobias mumbled again.

I pulled the covers up to my chin and kept my eyes on the window.

"Nothing."

~***~

"I say do it."

"What? I expected you to be my voice of reason," I said to Shelly. She and the twins had found the time to stop by and I was filling her in on my recent news.

Though Tobias hadn't seemed all that happy about the baby news at first, he was now singing a different tune. He asked me to marry him. He'd said that he knew that we hadn't been together all that long, but that he loved me, and now that I was having his child, he wanted to be there every step of the way…as my husband.

He asked me to be his wife and I wasn't sure what to say as of yet. I was wearing the ring but I hadn't given him an answer. I was confused. I didn't want him to want to marry be because I was pregnant, but he assured me that he loved me even before a baby became a part of the mix. He simply stated that the baby just made it clear to him that I was the one.

"I am being your voice of reason and here it is. You're old. In a little bit everything is going to start sagging, especially after you have that baby. You may have about five good years left. You've worked yourself to death. You've taken care of everyone but yourself. You left your job because you said that you wanted to live; well, live! Damn it live like you've never lived before! He wants to marry you. This is what you have been wanting. This is what you have been waiting on. You love him. He loves you. What's the problem?"

"We haven't known each other that long."

"Folks get married after a few months and stay married for twenty or thirty years all the time. Take a chance. Do the unexpected for once in your life. After all, there is always divorce. It isn't like it would be your first time at that rodeo."

This is crazy!

"Just do it," Shelly said and looked into the distance.

What's that face? Her facial expression said something, but I wasn't sure what it was. It seemed worried. It said that something was wrong or maybe that there was something that was bothering her. Whatever the look was, I didn't like it.

"Is everything okay with you?"

"Oh yeah, I'm fine."

"You and Brian are fine?"

"Never better. Anyway, so, are we planning a wedding or what?" Shelly forced a smile but I could see straight through it.

Hmm...I've got my eye on you sister!

I looked from Shelly, down at my hand and then touched my stomach. This is crazy! But I smiled and nodded my head. I'm getting married!

~***~

"Baby, I need you to sign here. And here. This stack of papers is the contract to the venue. And this paper says that we will provide our own minister. They want both signatures. Just put yours beside mine," he said reaching me a pen as I held a barbeque wing in my other hand.

"Dang, can it wait?" I said between chews.

"We need to lock it in. Don't want anyone to get our day. The other lines just need initials, I can do those. But you need to do your signature," he said as I scribbled my name next to his, realizing that he was right.

"Perfect. I'll go drop them off."

We were getting married in just two short weeks. We didn't want to wait until I was too far along into the pregnancy, and of course he wanted to be married before the baby came. Combined we had a lot of money in our savings, so it hadn't been hard to pay folks to get things done.

"I'll be right back."

Tobias headed out the door and I continued eating my food. As the days went by, I was becoming more and more excited about having a baby. I was going to be a good mother. I wasn't too far in but already I was imagining my baby's face and the sound of its cry. And I had a feeling that Tobias was going to make a great father too.

The doorbell chimed and I licked my fingers and headed to the door.

"Didn't I tell you to start calling before you come by?"

"I tried. It kept going to your voicemail," Ray said.

"Why are you here?"

"Well, I've been trying to find a way to tell you this, since I popped up that day. The day before my wedding. I woke up this morning, and I just couldn't go another day without telling you how I feel."

Uh oh. This was about to be trouble.

"Strawberry, I made a mistake. Agreeing for us to go our separate ways was a mistake. And getting remarried was a mistake too. So, I'm getting another divorce. I think I'm still in love with you Tiffany. To be honest, I don't think I ever stopped loving you. That's why I came by that day. I was supposed to have said that but when I saw you, I wanted to touch you. And then I wanted to kiss you. And then afterwards, I thought about how I had a beautiful woman expecting to walk down the aisle towards me the next day and I felt like a jerk that I had let things get so far. So I didn't say anything. But she isn't you. I was trying to fill a void. So, we're getting a divorce and I guess I just wanted to know if---,"

I held up my hand with the ring on it and he stopped talking abruptly.

"I'm getting married Ray, in two weeks. And I'm pregnant."

He swallowed, hard, and just looked at me. Briefly he glanced at my stomach and then he looked me directly in the eyes.

"Really? Uh, wow," he said. I just stared at him. "Were you serious when you said that you missed me? When you said that you missed us?"

I shook my head.

"No. Ray. I was just saying what I thought that you wanted to hear. I'm happy and I'm sorry your new marriage didn't work out but our divorce was the best thing for the both of us. I do wish you the best of luck," I said to him.

"I don't need luck. I just need you."

It was crazy that I went from no man for two whole years, to three men being interested in me, for whatever reasons, all at the same time.

I stared at Ray. I could tell that he was serious. And to be honest, if Tobias wasn't in the picture, I might give it a try. Just because I knew him. And he knew me. And that would mean that I didn't start over. And who knows, things might even be different, and we might would've worked the second time around. But Tobias was in the picture and Ray was just too late. He should have said what he'd had to say before he'd gotten married that day. He'd had his chance. He missed it.

"Don't marry him Strawberry. Marry me."

"I can't marry you, you're married remember?"

"Not for long. Work won't get in the way this time. I'll love you just like I did when we first met. I can give you what you need."

"Ray. I already have what I need."

I could tell that my statement hurt his feelings but it was the truth. Tobias was all the man that I'd ever need and more.

"Okay. Oh, by the way, that partial print actually did have a name attached to it, a "Delilah Philips". Name ring a bell?"

I shook my head no.

"And you said that the mugger was a man anyway right?"

I nodded. "Ray?" He ignored me.

"Well, she probably brushed up against it at the club or something. Anyway, well, congratulations," Ray said, but he stopped beside his patrol car.

"By the way, what's his name?"

"Who?"

"Your soon-to-be husband? What's his name?"

"Tobias. Tobias Fields."

Ray scoffed. Looked down at my stomach, and then got into his car and drove away.

Goodbye Ray.

~***~

"Is your little sister deaf?" Tobias asked.

"No. She just doesn't say much unless she's drunk. She's always been that way."

He nodded and he walked over towards Brian.

Shelly was having her husband a dinner in celebration of his new job.

I saw him smile, and I mean really smile, for the first time in months as Tobias headed away from the women and walked in his direction. The both headed to take a seat and watch TV.

I followed Shelly to the kitchen.

Something was wrong with her.

"What's wrong?"

"Nothing."

"I can tell."

She didn't say anything.

"What is it?"

She looked at me and I could tell that whatever she was about to say was some kind of secret or something.

She opened her mouth, but before she could say a word.

"Shelly!" Brian called, and she went running out of the kitchen in his direction.

Hmmm…

~***~

"Why have you never gotten married?"

"I guess I never found the one."

"And how do you know that she's the one?"

We were at a small counseling session with Mama's pastor. It was a requirement that he at least counseled us, once, in order for him to perform the ceremony.

"I knew that she was the one the moment that I laid eyes on her. She was like a breath of fresh air. She was everything that I ever dreamed of in a woman and in a wife. I know that she will make me happy and I'll do everything in my power to do the same," Tobias said.

I was sure that I couldn't put the smile on my face into words even if I tried. I had my reservations, but Tobias seemed so sure. He was sure that we were going to last forever, and if he was sure, that I had better get onboard and be sure too.

The pastor asked us a few more questions and then told us that he would see us on Saturday at the wedding. He walked us to the front of the church and Tobias headed to get the car.

"Mrs. Parks?"

"Yes Pastor?"

"Are you ready?"

"Yes. As ready as I'll ever be."

He nodded his head.

"He loves you. But something seems…"

"Seems what Pastor?"

"Rehearsed."

What did he mean by that?

"It was just some of the things that he said and the way that he'd said them. They were all wonderful things, but were they genuine? Does he show you unbreakable, unwavering love?"

"Oh, the way that he loves me, I can't even put it into words. He treats me like a queen. He really does."

"Well, sometimes even I get things wrong. Maybe he was just nervous. I think the union will be fine. Have a good night," he said as Tobias pulled up, and got out of the car to open my door.

I thought about the Pastor's words all the way home.

"I love you," Tobias said.

I stared deep into his eyes. I was looking for anything. I was looking for something. He smiled and looked at me with adornment.

Yeah. He was just nervous. The love that he had for me was real. I felt it and it showed.

"I love you too," I said and I meant it.

I was getting married!

****

Chapter SIX

"You look so beautiful," my baby sister April squealed and I was happy that she was showing some kind of excitement. But she was right. I did.

The dress was beautiful and hugged my curves just right. I didn't have a stomach as of yet, so that was a plus. I was so lucky that Mama could hem my dress in such short notice. Everything thing came together effortlessly. As though this day was really meant to be.

I stared at my reflection. My make-up was flawless. My hair was perfect. I looked happy. I looked ready.

But was I?

Tobias was a damn good man. He was everything that I'd ever wanted in a husband.

But what if we were rushing? What if it was too soon? What if we needed more time just to date and get to know each other? What if? What if? What if?

I briefly thought about Ray for some reason. I'd called him a few times; but he never answered or returned my calls. I hadn't expected him to confess his love for me and I would've been lying if I said that I hadn't been thinking about his words, because I had.

But the right thing to do was to follow my heart; and my heart belonged to Tobias.

Shelly came through the door and walked up to me.

"I just overheard Tobias on the phone. He's flipping out because his family is going to miss the wedding. Their plane is delayed and they are all stuck at the airport."

Uh oh. This must be a sign.

I had yet to meet his parents in person. I'd talked to them on the phone plenty of times, and his sister, but I hadn't got to meet them. They all lived in Louisiana and there was a good bit of his family members expecting to be at the wedding. I guess now they weren't going to make it. I just wondered how Tobias was going to feel about that.

"Your phone is ringing." I glanced down at my phone. It was Tobias.

"Hello."

"Hey. I just needed to hear your voice. I don't care what goes wrong today, as long as I marry the woman of my dreams and the woman that I'm madly in love with, everything else will be alright. The happiest moment of my life, other than watching our child be born when its time, is going to be me watching you walk down the aisle towards me. I love you and I'll be waiting for you."

Aww. I started to cry and everyone fussed at me for messing up my make-up.

"I love you."

"I love you too."

All of my doubts were suddenly gone and within the next thirty minutes or so, I became Mrs. Tobias Lucas Fields, and I was the happiest woman in the world.

The reception space was full of family and friends. Though Tobias's family hadn't made it, he'd invited lots of his colleagues. I tried to make my rounds to speak to them all. I'd been outside of Tobias's job a few times, waiting in the car for him as he ran in or something, but I had never met any of them. Most of them were married, so I was excited about possible double-dates. Making my rounds, I notice a familiar face, hanging onto the arm of a tall, dark, and chocolate man.

She saw me approaching and smiled.

"When he asked me to come to a wedding with him, I had no idea that it was yours." The lady that was the janitor at the company that I used to work for said. I was anxious to ask her if she'd heard any rumors about me in the work place. Though she was just the janitor, I'd seen her talking to a few of the workers, plenty of times, so I was sure that she'd heard something and I wanted to know what was being said.

"Thanks for coming. Do you still work there? Are people talking about me?"

She shook her head no.

"Not anymore. I was told to clean the office one day and noticed all of your things were gone. I was surprised and I made the statement that you loved your job, so I couldn't believe that you quit. And then one of the gentleman said that you didn't quit. He'd said that you had to go because you had been sleeping around with your boss and that his wife killed him for it."

Lies! I resigned! And I wasn't sleeping with him.

At her words, I saw Tobias cut his eye at me. I'd told him what I'd wanted him to know about the situation so he didn't need to hear any more of the conversation. He didn't need to know any of the details.

"That is a lie," I whispered, attempting to clear my name. "I resigned. I found out that I was pregnant and I was getting married, so I just wanted to enjoy life with my new family for a while. I did not sleep with my boss," I lied and told the truth at the same time.

She nodded her head and looked at my stomach.

"You're pregnant? You're not showing at all."

Of course I was really pregnant, but not as far along as I'd implied.

"Yes. I'm pretty small. But we're definitely having a baby."

Tobias walked over to me, kissed me, and said that he wanted to introduce me to a few more people. I was hoping that the janitor carried the story back to set the record straight. Not that I really cared, I just didn't want to be known as a slut.

Tobias and I talked to a few of his friends, and in the distance, I noticed a woman staring at me. Obviously, she was one of the workers of the venue. She had on all white and was standing near a table. I looked away for a moment but when I looked back at her, she just stared. She didn't even pretend not to be looking in my direction.

What is she looking at? Who is she?

"Baby, do you know that woman?"

Tobias looked at me.

"No. She looks like one of the employees," he said and he continued talking. Carrying on in conversation, by the next time I looked up, she was gone.

A few minutes later, my little sister April came running up to me.

"Come with me," she said grabbing my arm. We scurried to the ladies' bathroom. My sister Shelly followed us and April led us in.

"What in the hell?"

The bathroom was a mess! There was tissue everywhere. The mirror had been shattered. One of the stall doors was hanging off the hinges. Paper towels were all over the place and water. Lots and lots of water.

"What the hell happened in here?"

"I don't know. I was coming to use the bathroom. I heard a lot of noise. Some yelling but when I came in, the lady hung her head and walked out. I waited to see who she'd been yelling at, but no one else was in here. She was in here all alone. And then I saw all of this mess."

I looked around. Well, we were definitely going to have to pay for this. I looked down at the floor and I noticed the program from my wedding. The paper had been torn in little tiny pieces.

"Show me the lady that did this."

"I didn't really see her face. It happened so fast."

"When you see her, you'll know it. Show me."

I grabbed April and we headed back into the reception space. She looked over the crowd. She scanned the guests.

"I don't know. I don't think I see her."

I looked around for the woman that had been staring at me. The woman that was in the uniform but she was nowhere in sight.

"There! There she is going out the door!" April yelled over the music but by the time my eyes followed hers and her pointing finger, no one was there.

She was gone.

~***~

"You seem distant," I mentioned to Tobias as we boarded the plane the next day for our honeymoon.

"Do I? I was just thinking is all."

"About what?"

"Forever. With you." I blushed as he kissed me. But just as we took our seats, the announcer spoke.

"I'm sorry, but there seems to be a situation. We need everyone to get off of the plane."

Everyone looked confused and started to chatter. We made our way back to the waiting area where we learned that an anonymous tip came in that Flight 104, our flight, had a bomb on the plane.

Officials came from everywhere and we were told that we were all going to have to be given different flights. After waiting around for three hours and becoming restless, and with the airline offering free travels, the next three times we fly, first class, as a result of rescheduling, Tobias suggested that we go home.

I was so irritated. My pregnancy was whopping my ass and I was hoping to be half-way to a beach by now.

"I have two weeks off. Let's reschedule and leave Wednesday. I'll call the hotels and everything in the morning," Tobias said and I shook my head. In disbelief that something like that happened, exhausted, within the next hour or so, I was fast asleep.

"Late dinner?" Tobias suggested once I was awake. I was starving so I nodded, got myself together and within minutes we were on our way to the closest restaurant. I would have rather been relaxing on a beaches of Punta Cana, enjoying our honeymoon, but in due time.

"Thank you baby," I said smiling as I took a seat.

"Um, you look good enough to eat," Tobias said, being nasty.

"Well, you can eat me all you want later. But right now, I need to feed this baby."

His face expression at the word "baby" seemed to change. It was as though he'd gone from happy, to sad, in an instant. But he tried to disguise it.

The waiter took our order and we chatted about our wedding and I told him about the bathroom incident.

"Hello, how are you doing?"

I turned around to see a little old lady.

Tobias smiled.

"Mrs. Franklin, how are you doing?"

"I'm doing really good. My daughter talked me into coming out to dinner. You know that I don't like to eat out. I don't trust people with my food. Not eating out is how I've been able to stick around this long," she said.

I smiled at her.

She had to be in her 80's.

"Was your wife busy tonight?" she said, looking at me as though I'd done something wrong.

"Excuse me?" Tobias said.

"Your wife? Was she too busy to come to dinner tonight?"

"Mrs. Franklin, this is my wife."

"No it isn't."

"Yes, it is. See," he said showing her my ring.

"What happened to the other wife?"

"Michelle wasn't my wife Mrs. Franklin. We were just engaged. It didn't work out."

"Oh, forgive me," she said to me and then Tobias stood to give her a hug, and she headed on her way.

"Michelle? I never heard you mention a Michelle in our conversations. And you never told me that you were engaged," I eyed him.

"You heard me call her Micki. Micki is Michelle."

I did remember him telling me about Micki, but he still didn't tell me that they had been engaged.

"And why didn't you guys work out, again? Refresh my memory."

"We didn't work out. That's pretty much it."

"No, I want to know why."

"Tiffany, she just wasn't the one for me." I could tell by the way that he said it that the conversation was over.

But only for now.

~***~

"How is the married life treating you so far?"

"I'm so happy Shelly. I don't want to come back."

We were on our last day of our late honeymoon and I was really enjoying myself. Everything was so beautiful and I wanted to stay forever, with Tobias, and in a few months our baby.

"I wish we could stay forever."

"Uh, no, I would love to be able to see my niece or nephew often. I've been going by and checking on your house like you told me. Everything looks fine. I've been checking your mail, but you haven't had one piece of mail since you've been gone."

"Really? I always have a lot of mail. Are you sure?"

"Yep. Not one piece. I don't know. Maybe check into it when you get back."

We got off of the phone and I stared at Tobias on the balcony. He had been out there for a while, talking business I suppose. Even though he was on vacation, his phone hadn't stopped ringing. With my permission, finally he excused himself and took the call. But I was about to interrupt him.

I walked outside and I fell to my knees.

Tobias stopped talking and looked at me. He tried to push me away, but since he was smiling, I knew that he wanted it, so I headed for his main missile.

He tried to talk, but my sucking took his breath away and without even saying bye, he hung up the phone and closed his eyes. He relaxed and I "rocked his mic".

Hey, might as well end our honeymoon with a bang.

~***~

I just don't know what happened.

For the first month of our marriage, I felt as though I was in Heaven on Earth. We were both so happy. We couldn't keep our hands off of each other and everything was just so perfect.

But...now...something was wrong.

"Are you hungry?"

"Nope."

"Do you want something to drink?"

"Didn't I say no!" Tobias yelled at me, causing me to jump.

"What in the hell is wrong with you Tobias? Why are you acting this way?"

"You! You are what's wrong with me!"

Tobias yelled and then he headed out the door.

Here lately, he had been acting so rude and obnoxious, for no reason at all. He wasn't acting like himself, and thinking about his behavior, I started to cry.

I started to call his phone over and over again. Of course he didn't pick up but today, he wasn't getting off that easy. Grabbing my keys, I headed to find him. I headed to his job, his car wasn't there. So, I headed to his house.

For Sale.

I was surprised to see a for sale sign in the front yard.

When did he put his house up for sale?

And why hadn't he told me?

I called him again, but he didn't answer and he didn't answer for the rest of the day. In fact, that night, he didn't even bother to come home.

The next day, I called him a thousand times and still no answer. I'd gone by his job again, and he still wasn't there.

He wasn't going to work and he wasn't answering his phone, so where was he?

I was hoping that nothing had happened to him although he was being a jackass. He had never done this before and he wasn't going to start this bull crap either!

Or he would lose his wife, before I'd even gotten used to using my last name.

I ate dinner alone and once the clock struck 8:30, I called Tobias again. This was my last time calling and if he didn't answer, I was going to leave him a voicemail telling him that I wanted a divorce.

"Hello?"

"Hello? Where in the hell are you! So you think this acceptable? You think that you can leave for almost two days and not call your wife? Who does that? I'm not dealing with this shit Tobias! I'm pregnant and I'm not dealing with this!"

"Shut up, I'm on my way," he said.

"No you're not," a voice said in the background. It was faint, and low, but I'd heard it. And it belonged to a woman.

"What?"

"What, what? I said that I'm on my way. Are you okay? Do you need anything from the store?" He asked as though he hadn't done anything wrong.

"No. Who are you with?"

"No one. I'm in the store. I was in the mood for something sweet, so I stopped to get me something and then I was coming home."

I know I heard a woman's voice but now everything was quiet.

"Whatever Tobias," I growled and hung up the phone.

Had he been with another woman?

Maybe the voice belonged to a woman in the store that was talking to someone else. But since he had been showing me a different side of him lately, I wasn't going to put anything by him. Who knows what the hell he was doing or where he really was. But I swore on my unborn child's life that I wasn't going to put up with nonsense.

Ray and I fell out of love, but never did I have to worry about him cheating on me with another woman.

Never did he get so angry to where he just didn't come home.

I thought long and hard for a few minutes and then a knock came to the door and I headed towards it.

"Who is it?"

"Pizza," they said.

Pizza? I didn't order pizza. I placed my hand on the knob but something told me to look through the peep hole first. And I was glad that I did.

Someone was standing there, wearing a black mask. It looked homemade. They were dressed in all black and once they scratched their nose, I could see that they were also wearing gloves.

They knocked again.

"Pizza."

My heart started racing and I dialed 9-1-1.

I had no idea what to think.

The door knob started to wiggle and I started to panic.

"Hello? Someone is trying to break into my house," I whispered. The wiggling stopped and after the operator told me that someone was on the way, I hung up the phone and looked through the hole.

The person in the mask was gone.

I thought I was in the clear. I thought that everything was fine, but I was positive that these incidents weren't coincidental.

"Was it a man or a woman?"

"I'm not sure. I think a man, but I could tell that they were trying to disguise their voice so I'm not sure."

Tobias jumped out of the car before he even put it into park once he pulled up to see me talking to the police.

"What happened? What's wrong?"

I filled him in and continued to talk to the police. All of a sudden, another police car pulled up and Ray got out of it.

What was he doing here? How did he know?

He talked to some of the other officers and then he asked if he could talk to me alone.

"Are you okay?"

"Yeah. How did you know I called the police?"

"What happened?"

"Someone was trying to get in. He or she, was wearing a mask."

"What is going on around here lately?" Ray asked.

"I was wondering the same thing. These last few months' things have been crazy. It seems as though someone is out to get me or something. It seems like something bigger is going on around me and I just, I just don't know what to do. I'm scared Ray."

I could tell that he wanted to hug me but of course he didn't.

"Do you think that Tobias has anything to do with any of this?"

"What? No. Why would he?"

"It was just a question. Tiffany, there is something that I need to tell you."

I looked at him. Last time he said that, he confessed his love for me. I wondered what was about to come out of his mouth now.

"Tobias Fields isn't his real name."

"What?"

"Your husband. Tobias Field's isn't his real name. I tried to check him out. Just to check and there are only two Tobias Field's within 100 miles from here; and he isn't one of them."

"What?"

"Why would he lie about his name? Don't you think that's strange?"

"Ray, what right do you have to run a search on my husband? Don't you think that I know his name?"

"He isn't who he says that he is Tiffany. At least not by that name. If he is lying about his name, what else is he lying about? And think back, think back to the mugging. Had you met him yet? When did all of these things start happening."

"No. Yes. But we weren't talking or anything. I don't have to explain anything to you. Oh, I see what this is. You just don't want me to be happy. This isn't about me. Or about Tobias. This is about you. Because you still love me and you can't accept that I've found happiness. Ray, you were too late. So get over it! Instead of trying to start rumors about my husband!"

"It's not like that."

"Sure it is. Just like apparently you're keeping some kind of tabs on me too, since you're here. How do I know that it wasn't you at the door?" I scowled Ray and he looked as though he wanted to strangle me. Before he could say a word, I stormed away from him and headed back towards Tobias who was waiting for me.

"Everything okay?

"Yeah. Everything is fine."

"Do you guys have anywhere else that you can go? You've stated that there have been a few incidents, so maybe it's time to get away from this place for a while."

I remembered that I'd seen Tobias's house up for sale. He hadn't even told me. But he was about to tell me right now.

"Yes. My husband has a house, we can…"

"Actually, I don't."

I looked at Tobias and the police officer stepped away.

"What do you mean you don't have a house?"

"Uh, I rented it out."

"You rented it out? Or are your selling it?"

He looked at me catching on that I knew that he hadn't told me about his plans for his house.

"Either way, we can't stay there," he said.

I stared at him.

Who did I marry?

~***~

"This is a courtesy call. We are calling just to make sure everything is okay when large sums are taken out of an account. Since your husband made the withdrawal, we tried to call him first. But since we couldn't reach him, we were calling you."

We'd joined our accounts the week that we were married. Of course I had more money, but he had a good bit of his own and since we were getting married, we both agreed that it didn't really matter whose money was whose.

There was plenty, and to be honest, I hadn't even known how much I had until we'd gone to the bank. I never really checked my accounts the way that most people did. I just knew there was plenty of money there, so I didn't check it as often as I probably should have. Every bill that I had, was set up as direct debits, so I never manually did anything. Even when I quit my job, I calculated in my head around how much I should have, and went from there.

He had plenty of his own money, so I wasn't really worried. But I was just a little bit curious.

"How much was the withdrawal?"

"$50,000."

$50,000? For what? What the hell did he need that much money for?

I instructed the banker to notify me from now on anytime anything over $500 dollars was taken out of our account. I also informed her that I was on my way to the bank to do a little moving around with the money myself.

I headed to the bank to open a savings account that Tobias was to know nothing about. I withdrew a couple thousands instead of transferring them. Something was telling me to play it smart so that was exactly what I was going to do.

Leaving the bank, I had so much on my mind.

Tobias used to be an open book, now he seemed to be hiding things from me and I was starting to feel like there was something about him that I missed.

A few hours later, Tobias walked in. Since we'd been back from the honeymoon, I noticed that he hadn't been as busy as he normally was. To be honest, he had barely even been going in to work.

Something was going on, so I felt as though it was time that I found out.

"So, when were you going to tell me that you lost your job? When did you get fired?"

"What?"

"Don't play dumb with me! I already know. You don't work there anymore. So, when were you going to tell me?"

Hell, of course I didn't know if he had been fired or not, but I was trying to find out. All I knew was that it was something.

Tobias sat across from me with a smirk on his face.

"Well, if you figured out that I was "fired", you should have figured out that I never worked there in the first place," he said and sat back into the chair to get a good view of my reaction.

"What?"

"I never worked there Strawberry."

I was hoping to get the truth, but I wasn't expecting this.

"What do you mean you never worked there?"

"Just what I said."

"So, you haven't worked this whole time?"

"Nope. At least not there anyway."

My mouth was wide open.

"Then where do you work?"

"I'm a business man."

"A business man? Don't play with me Tobias!"

He laughed in a crazy sort of way.

"So the job, the calls, the phone, the conference trip, it was all a lie?"

"It depends on how you look at it. I was working, but not where and how you thought I was."

"And your colleagues at our wedding?"

"Friends. If you had paid attention, we never talked about work. I only told you that they were colleagues. I never once mentioned that we worked together in front of them."

Well, I'll be damned! I wanted to say so many things but I couldn't get them out fast enough.

"All those times you were rushing to work. Or staying late because of a problem. It was all lies?"

"Some of them. But as I said, it depends on how you look at it. But enough about me, what were you doing at the bank today?"

I was still stuck on the fact that he'd been lying about his job the whole time. I wondered what kind of "business" he was involved in and now I wondered if the break-ins were related to him, and had nothing to do with me.

What if he was involved in something illegal?

"Why were you at the bank Strawberry?"

"I should be asking you that. Why did you take $50,000 out of our account?"

"I'm working on something. I didn't know that I had to tell you when I got money out of the bank. It's my money in there too."

"Yes, it is. But if you were lying about working in stocks, then where did the money come from?"

"It doesn't matter. It's mine. That's all that matters."

"Why can't I know the truth? Why are you keeping things from me?"

"What's with all of the questions? The best thing for you to do is to shut-up, and mind your business."

"Who do you think you are talking to? You are the one that has been lying. You are the one hiding things from me. You are the one acting crazy!"

"Look, stop with all the yapping and make yourself useful and go fix me some food."

Tobias walked away from me as I started to curse.

At that moment I realized that I should have listened to my gut. I shouldn't have listened to him. I shouldn't have listened to Shelly. I should have listened to my gut. I didn't know him well enough to marry him. We were rushing into something because I was pregnant and now I was convinced that it was the wrong thing to do.

I thought about the Pastor saying that Tobias's responses seemed rehearsed. I guess I was so blinded by love that I couldn't see it, but from the looks of it, he was right. Tobias had been saying all of the right things, but had he meant them? I wasn't so sure.

"Is Tobias your real name?" I screamed after him. Out of all of the cursing that I had done, that question caught his attention.

"What?"

"Is Tobias your real name?"

"Of course. Why would you ask me that?"

"Hell, apparently, I don't really know YOU," I said and took a seat on the couch. "I suggest that you, whoever you really are, go into the kitchen and fix yourself something to eat or your ass is going to starve. And from here on out, I wouldn't eat a damn thing that I cooked if I were you, because I can assure you that whatever I put in your plate, was put there on purpose, and may potentially be deadly. Opps," I said to him sarcastically.

He looked at me like I was crazy, but I turned away from him, and silently…I cried.

~***~

"I don't want this baby anymore."

Shelly looked at me.

"Is it too late to have an abortion?"

"I think you can have one up to four months, maybe more, these days, but why are you even talking about that? What's wrong?"

My emotions took over and I started to cry.

"Tobias is acting weird. He has changed. He's being rude. He's being lying to me from the very beginning and I have a feeling that he isn't who he says that he is."

Shelly looked at me as I cried.

"I feel like I don't know him at all."

Shelly held me for a second and then she pulled away from me and looked into my eyes.

"Brian knows Tobias."

I looked at Shelly confused.

"After you introduced Tobias to us, they started to communicate. But I would sneak and listen to their conversations and I could tell that they already knew each other. I overheard Brian say, "Remember when we…" So they had to have known each other, prior to the initial introduction."

What?

"I wouldn't be surprised if Brian didn't send Tobias in your direction."

"What like set us up on purpose? But why?"

"I don't know why, but why else would they know each other and not mention it? Then, Brian started telling me not to come over here and started complaining that I was over here too much and in the way. Whenever I would call he would rush me off of the phone or get mad. And…"

"What?"

"He told me to convince you to marry Tobias. He already knew that Tobias was going to propose. He asked me if you were going to do it, and when I told him that you were confused, he told me to talk you into doing it. He'd said that you needed a husband and that you would listen to me. At first, I thought that he just wanted you to be married so that he could have me all to himself, but its more than that."

What?

"Shelly, something isn't right."

"I know. And it gets worse. The other day, I accidentally knocked over the trash can in the garage and this fell out," Shelly said and pulled the mask out of her purse.

It was a black homemade mask, just like the one that the person had been wearing when they tried to get inside of my house not too long ago.

"Wait a minute. Wait a minute. What? So are you telling me that Brian was the one at the door? The masked man that tried to break in?"

"I don't know but it sure looks that way." Shelly was shaking.

"It's going to be okay."

"What should I do?"

Hell, the question was what was I going to do? Obviously something was going on and it didn't look as though things were going to turn out good for me.

"Nothing. You don't do or say anything. I don't want you apart of any of this."

"He was too good to be true," Shelly said.

She was right. He was. I always thought that eventually Tobias would slack off a little and settle into our relationship, but I never thought that he had some other side to him. Not one like this. Not one that seemed to be vindictive and obnoxious. Not one as evil as he had been lately.

"At the end of the day, you are my sister. My flesh and blood. I got your back; even if I have to go up against my husband. I think maybe I need to get rid of him anyway," Shelly said, grabbing my hand.

This is exactly what I get. I'd always known that what goes around, comes around, even if the blow hits you on a totally different level.

Hello, Karma…I've been waiting for you.

~***~

"I'm Nurse Jacky. What's been going on?"

"I've been having some pain."

"Are you bleeding?"

"No. Just some pain."

She touched my stomach.

I was at the emergency room…by myself.

I didn't know where Tobias was, and I didn't care. I woke up having pains, so I drove myself to the hospital.

"Okay, a doctor will be in here soon. Oh, by the way, are you allergic to any medicines?"

"Yes. Penicillin."

"Okay," she said.

She walked out and I laid still for a second.

I felt like I was in one of my nightmares. I just wanted to wake up. I just wanted it to be over.

Tobias flipped flopped so much that I'd started calling him Tobias One and Tobias Two. I would ask him which one he planned on being for that day. He still wasn't acting like the man that I married, but some days, he wasn't as bad. It was as if it was taking all of his energy to be mean to me, so it seemed as though some days, he took a break. But the very next day, he would be right back at it.

He was doing the weirdest stuff too.

Cutting the tops off of all of my socks. Cutting the cord on my blow dryer, knowing that I was washing my hair in the shower. He would leave mess, all over the house and watch me clean it up.

He was just nothing like the man that I thought I'd married. And the sudden change had me devastated.

"Knock. Knock. Hello, I'm Nurse Danielle. I'm your nurse tonight."

"What happened to Nurse Jacky?"

"Who?"

"Nurse Jacky? She was just in here."

"I'm sorry, but we don't have a Nurse Jacky."

Huh?

****

CHAPTER SEVEN

Tobias said a smart remark and threw his cup full of drink out of his car window, purposely in my direction.

That's it!

Before I could stop myself and forgetting that I was pregnant, I literally lunged my body through the driver's side window and started swinging.

"Move Strawberry! You better move!" Tobias screamed, trying to shield himself. Surprisingly, I thought that he would have hit me back considering that he was such a jackass lately, but he didn't. I guess physical abuse wasn't his thing; just mental and emotional abuse was.

He had been stressing me out so bad lately that I didn't know whether I was coming or going most days. He complained about everything and gave me the hardest time. Whenever he was home. It had become the normal not to see him for 24 hours at a time. Those were the best hours of my life. I'd even changed the locks one day while he was gone, but he picked it.

I'd called the police to put him out, but they said some bull about giving him a 30-day notice. I just couldn't get rid of his ass.

Out of breath, I finally pushed away from him.

"I don't care where you go. Or what you do. Don't bring your ass back here! Ever! This is over!" I took off my ring and he laughed.

"You can't divorce me Strawberry."

"Oh yes I can and I will."

"Like I said, you can't divorce me."

"Watch me."

"Well, if you do, you'll lose everything."

"What? What the hell are you talking about?"

"Remember those papers that I had you sign? When I said that the venue for the wedding needed your signature? I lied. That's not what those papers were."

It felt as though my body had been overtaken by Hell's fire!

"One of them was our little agreement that whoever initiates the divorce, gets nothing. So if you divorce me, I get everything. The money, the house, even your car."

"What! You tricked me? I'll beat you in court."

"No you won't. They are notarized and my lawyer has a copy."

I couldn't believe this! He was a crook! And he was trying to force me to stay married to him?

"Who are you?"

"I'm your husband Strawberry," he said with a smile and he put his car in reverse.

"What about the other paper? That day you had me sign two pieces of paper. What was the other paper?" I was so angry that I was crying, but Tobias was smiling.

"That's for me to know. And for you to find out. I'll be back later…baby," he said and he drove away.

I stood in my driveway in tears. I was trying to figure out what was going on. I was trying to make sense of everything he had just said.

He was trying to make me stay married to him, yet he wasn't anything like the man that he'd pretended to be. He was treating me like shit, so why not want a divorce?

Obviously he didn't want this marriage for real, so why try to leave me with nothing if I didn't stay?

I looked down at the ring that was on the pavement.

This marriage was one big joke.

Why did he do this? Why did he choose me?

Feeling sharp pains in my stomach, I headed inside of the house. I sat still and tried to figure out my next move. I needed to see these papers that he'd had me sign, I wondered if they would stick. And now that he revealed what they were, it seemed as though he was trying to force me towards divorce.

He wanted everything. He doesn't love me. And I was convinced that he never had.

But he wasn't taken what I'd worked so hard for. I'd lost everything behind that job. I'd lost a marriage, friends, self-respect and so much more over the years, and the one thing that the job had been good for was money. And he thought that he was just going to come in and take it?

Over my dead body! He wasn't getting a dime!

And I was going to make sure of that.

I thought for a little while longer. I needed to see those papers. I needed to know what they said.

He had to have a copy…right?

And I didn't stand in front of a notary so who ever notarized them deserved to be fined, penalized, or something. But that might work in my favor.

I headed to our bedroom. I started going through his stuff. He had to have his copy of the paperwork somewhere.

I searched until I was out of breath and still came up with nothing. But what I did do was throw his clothes out of the bedroom window. It had started to rain, so I'd decided to let Mother Nature wash them. If I'd had the energy, I would have done more than that, but that was the best that I could do to get under his skin at the moment.

Headed back into the living room, I knew that I needed a plan. I knew that I had to be two steps ahead of him. He was up to something.

Something strange was going on with him and Brian. I still wasn't sure what Brian had to do with all of this, or if that was him at the door that night, but if it was, I knew there was something that I wasn't seeing.

I called Shelly, but she didn't pick up. She didn't really know what to think of her husband these days.

I thought about Tobias and then I remembered what my ex-husband had said to me.

He'd said that Tobias wasn't his real name. With everything going on now, I felt like a fool for being mean to him and not believing him. Ray was only trying to help. And now, I was sure that he was right.

I didn't know who in the hell Tobias really was and at this point, I felt like I had no choice but to try to find out. But I was going to need some help. I was going to need Ray's help.

I knew that Ray wouldn't want to talk to me, but I went out on a limb and called him anyway.

But just as I suspected, he didn't answer.

~***~

"Who are you talking to?"

"Nobody," Tobias said.

"Who is nobody?"

He ignored me as though I hadn't said a word.

Just as he was about to say goodbye, I snatched his phone.

"Hello? Who is this?"

"Who is this?" she said.

"This is wife."

She giggled and then she hung up. Tobias stood up and snatched his phone from my hands.

"Who was that?"

"Nobody."

"So you're having an affair?"

"Nope."

"Well who was she?"

"Nobody important."

He walked towards the kitchen and I followed him screaming.

"Why won't you just leave?"

"Why won't you just leave me? It'll make things easier."

"What does that mean?"

"Nothing."

"This is my house! Get out!"

"What's yours is mine Mrs. Fields."

"You're not running me out of my house."

"Then stay. I never asked you to go. But I'm not going anywhere until…"

He stopped talking abruptly. Until what?

I slammed my hands down on the island in the middle of the kitchen.

Tobias just looked at me.

I wanted to cuss and fuss but it seemed as though my body wouldn't let me. Mentally, emotionally, physically, I was tired.

I took a seat and rubbed my four-month belly.

"You aint lost that damn baby yet?"

What did he just say to me?

Who says that to a pregnant lady? What kind of man says that to his wife?

"I would have thought that by now, you would have lost it. After all that has been going on."

I looked into his eyes and I saw that he was serious.

"Is this what this is all about? Because you want me to lose the baby? Is this why you have been treating like this?"

Tobias didn't say anything.

All he'd had to say was that he didn't want it. He was the one that suggested that we get married and become a family, not me.

"I'll fix it."

"What?"

"I've heard that now you can have an abortion up to four or five months, I'll fix it."

I was crying so hard that I was starting to choke on my tears. This is not how I thought things were going to be. I thought that I was going to be happy. I thought that I was in love.

"Don't cry Strawberry. I love you," he said.

"Lies! It was all lies! You don't love me. And you never did."

"That's not true."

"Then what is true? What is the truth Tobias?"

"Like I said, I do love you," was all that he said and he hummed as a way to drown out the sound of my sniffles.

Later that night, I watched him sleep.

He'd fallen asleep on the couch. His phone was on the table, vibrating. Though he'd gotten rid of the "work" phone, now the personal phone rung just as much as that one did.

I picked it up.

Of course it had a lock on it now, but I waited to see if it was going to ring again so that I could answer it.

It did, but the call came in as Private.

I answered anyway.

"Hello?"

They didn't say anything.

"Who are you? How much can I pay you to tell you everything that I need to know about Tobias? I know that you know something. What will it cost me for the truth?"

I waited, but they didn't respond so eventually I hung up. I watched the phone but no one ever called back. The phone didn't ring for the rest of the night.

And that was a first.

~***~

"I don't want you here," I said to Tobias. He looked at me as if I was speaking a foreign language or something.

"I'm not leaving."

"You don't even want the baby, so why come?"

"If you're going to do this why let you do it alone?"

We were at the abortion clinic. I found out that you could now have them up to twenty weeks and I was only seventeen and a half.

Yes. I was showing and I was even feeling movement. Yes, it was a real baby; if that was even appropriate to say, but it had all of its body parts. Unlike the first two times, I'd only been a few weeks.

But it was clear that Tobias didn't want the baby, at all, and that the whole time he had been hoping that somehow I lost it. My guess was that he'd used the pregnancy to get me to marry him. That had to be the only reason that he'd pretended to want the baby in the first place.

It was killing me inside to know what I was about to do. Unlike the other times, this time, now, I wanted my baby with all of my heart. I wanted to see it's face. I wanted to hold the baby in my arms, next to my heart.

But I was so stressed. I was so confused. I was so tired and I just felt like having the baby was one more thing that would keep Tobias around, and I just wanted him to go away. I just wanted him far, far, away from me.

All the love that I'd felt for him, seemed like a distant memory. I couldn't say that I didn't love him anymore; even though I didn't want to. I would be lying if I said that my love for him was completely gone. But I could say that I felt deceived and because of my feelings, I felt a sense of hatred towards him too.

Getting rid of the baby was the best thing to do.

When it was all said and done, I didn't want anything to do with Tobias. And I didn't want a baby in the middle of it. I was going to file for a divorce so that my lawyer could get a look at these papers that he'd made me sign. There had to be a way around them. And I would hire one of the best lawyers in town to help me beat him.

He wasn't taking my money. He wasn't taking my house. I'd burn that bitch down to the ground before I let him have it.

I had been stashing thousands of dollars, mad money, in my secret savings account and in my little sister's account, every other day.

Whether Tobias noticed or not, I didn't care. But he never asked and of course he didn't know where it was going.

"Just leave."

"No. It's my baby too."

I gave him a look that could have sent him into cardiac arrest. He was such a freaking joke!

After sitting there in complete silence for another thirty minutes or so, finally, it was time.

"I just want to take a look first," the doctor said as he pulled the baby up on the screen.

"Wow. Look at him. He's all over the place," he said.

"He?" Tobias repeated.

"I'm sorry. You didn't know the sex of the baby?"

I stared at the screen as the baby moved around. I felt like dying. That was my son on that screen and I was never going to get the chance to meet him. Tears rolled angrily down my face. I was heartbroken.

"Get up."

I looked at Tobias. He was crying too. And I'm talking about he was crying as though his Mama had just died or as if he had just been told that he only had a few days to live.

"I said get up."

Tobias grabbed me by the hand and the doctor looked confused.

"Come on."

"What?" I was crying my eyes out. I just stood there. Tobias wiped my face and then reached for my hand.

"Come on."

"There's no refund," the doctor said as Tobias opened the door and led the way. But neither of us looked back.

~***~

Tobias and I walked around for three days barely saying a word to each other. He seemed to be somewhere else, though he was there. I couldn't explain it, but he just seemed out of it.

And he wasn't being mean to me anymore. He was actually being very nice. He wasn't staying out and he was coming home every night. Though he barely spoke to me at all, when he did, he wasn't being disrespectful.

It was clear to me that he'd been trying to stress me out on purpose, but now the sad part was that I didn't know what to believe. I didn't know what was lies and what was the truth. I didn't know if he'd just said things to intentionally hurt me and cause me stress, or if he had meant them. I really just didn't know.

But though he seemed to be acting like the Tobias that I first met, I still didn't trust him. With everything that had gone on and all of the little discoveries, I didn't want anything to do with him. I still wanted to get as far away from him as possible. Somehow, someway, the baby and I were just going to have to come up missing.

"Is he moving?"

"Yes."

It seemed as though finding out that the baby was a boy had done something to Tobias. It seemed to have touched his heart. It seemed to have made him want to be a father more than ever. But hey, what man doesn't want a son? I'd heard my father beg my Mama for another baby once he'd had three girls, but she'd told him that her ovaries were no longer in service and that if he ever wanted to touch her again, he had to get a vasectomy. So, he did.

"Can I feel it?"

I looked at him as to tell him if he touched me I would stab him but I rolled my eyes and shrugged my shoulders instead. He smiled as the baby moved around a little.

"Hey son," he whispered.

I almost smiled but I caught myself. He was the enemy. If I had my way, my son would never even get to meet him.

"We need to talk," I said.

"We will," Tobias said as he stood up, grabbed his keys and headed out the front door.

I rolled my eyes and checked my phone.

Shelly had called me a hundred times in the last two days, but whenever I called her back, she never answered.

I had five missed calls from her from an hour ago and a text message that said, "Call me back, it's important".

I called her a few more times, but she never picked up. I sat the phone beside of me as I laid on the couch to take a nap. I left it on vibrate. Hopefully if she called, I would hear it.

I used to be scared to stay home alone, let alone trying to sleep. But now I was more scared to sleep when Tobias was in the house with me. There were plenty of times that I thought that he was going to do something crazy. But he never did.

By the next time that I opened my eyes, it was around five o'clock in the evening. Tobias still wasn't home. And I still didn't care.

Yawning, I grabbed my phone to head to check the mailbox. I had tons of missed calls from Shelly again and one new voicemail. I pressed the #1 and waited to hear what she had to say. Looking at the mail, I paused when I heard her breathing.

"Strawberry, call me. I have something to tell you. Brian and Tobias---" Bang! Bang! Bang!

Hearing the noise, I dropped the phone.

Immediately I started to cry and scream.

Those were gun shots! Those were gun shots!

I grabbed my stomach, and I heard a car pull in behind me.

Ray.

I shook my head.

"No! No! No!"

Ray hadn't talked to me and wouldn't answer my calls so if he was here now, something was wrong. I could see it on his face.

"No! She's not dead. Please don't tell me that she's dead."

Ray reached out his arms.

"I wanted to be the one to deliver the news. Shelly was shot. She's in the hospital, but she isn't responding. It doesn't look good for her. I tried to call but it only goes to voicemail."

So, she wasn't dead. As long as she wasn't dead.

I tried to calm myself down and Ray waited patiently. He allowed me to cry, and then breathe. Breathe and then cry. And then finally I was able to speak.

"What happened to her? I mean, who shot her?"

"No one knows. She was leaving work, and all we know is that gunshots were fired from an older model vehicle, red, and it didn't have a license plate. The few witnesses didn't see the driver and it happened so fast that they couldn't even remember what kind of car it was. But we are checking all surrounding cameras. We will do everything that we can to find who did this to her."

Now, I was crying on Ray's shoulder.

Who did this to my sister?

Glancing at my phone through my tears, I remembered Shelly's voicemail.

"Ray?"

He just looked at me as I squatted to get my phone.

"Listen."

He didn't say anything. He just listened.

"Somebody did this to her. I think she found out something that she wasn't supposed to know. You were right. Tobias isn't who he says that he is. And maybe Brian isn't either. One of them did something to her, I just know it. I just know it," I cried even harder than I was before.

Ray looked around.

"Tiffany. Tobias isn't his real name."

"I know."

Well of course it wasn't. I listened attentively.

"In my spare time, I've still been checking into him. It's not because I'm jealous. It's because I care. It took some time. A lot of digging, and a lot of going through photos of past arrests that matched his height, weight, and other physical similarities, but I found something. I've found him, in the database, twice, under two different names and I'm pretty sure that neither of those names are his real names either. He must work with someone to change his identity and whoever it is, is really good. The names, aliases have birth certificates, social security numbers, credit scores; they have it all."

Immediately I thought of Brian. He was a computer genius. Surely, he could create a fake person. Surely he knew how to get someone a new identity and even hack into a few systems to enter a person and make it look like they really exist. I was sure of it. Maybe that was the connection. Maybe that's how he and Tobias knew each other. Maybe they worked together.

"On one of the fake names, Benjamin Lewis, he was brought in for questioning on his wife's murder."

"Wife? Tobias has never been married."

"Maybe "Tobias" hasn't; but "Benjamin" has. It's him. I saw the photo. Same man, just a different name."

I started to shake my head.

"Anyway, the wife was very wealthy. This was in Denver, Colorado. Her family owned a lot of stuff down there. Well, she turned up dead and they thought maybe he had done it; accept he was thousands of miles away on an airplane at the time. They said that there was no way that he could have done anything to her and of course he said that he would never hurt her. He said that he loved her. And there wasn't anything connecting him to it either. No crazy random calls to set it up. Nothing. He really appeared to be innocent. The case is still unsolved, but they are positive in that precinct that the husband had nothing to do with it.

Anyway, he walked away with over five million dollars. Her accounts and her life insurance policy."

Life insurance policy?

Was that the other piece of paper that he'd tricked me into signing? He said some of the pages needed initials, and just that one signature. It could've been a policy. Hell, it could've been anything.

"After that, Benjamin Lewis fell off of the face of the earth. No one ever saw him again. In a way, if I was being falsely accused of my wife's murder, I guess I could see leaving the state and maybe even changing my name and starting over. I could almost understand it…until I found him with another name. George West. He was in the system for a DWI. And he lived in Texas. No one has seen or heard of him in years either. He was married too, but that wife didn't turn up dead. They had a rather quiet divorce and I couldn't get much information on it. All I know is that she was wealthy too. It all seems a little fishy to me."

I didn't know what to say. I didn't know what to think.

"I'm not saying that he's a murderer or anything and honestly, he doesn't fit the profile. But I am saying that he's hiding something and whatever it is, it's big. So just be careful. Maybe you and the baby should get away from him."

"He won't let me."

He was right but since we'd found out that we were having a boy, Tobias has been on me like a hawk. Even when he wasn't around, he always seemed to find out where I was or where I had been. Getting away from him wasn't going to be easy.

"Do you think that I'm in danger Ray?"

"Honestly, I don't know Strawberry. I just," Ray stopped.

"What?"

"I don't want to see anything happen to you. As I said, I've never stopped caring about you. If you ever need me, call me. If I find out something else, you will be the first to know. Do you want a ride to the hospital?"

"No. I want to be the one to tell my Mama and sister. I'll drive. So that I can pick them up on the way. Does her husband know?"

"Of course. He had to be informed first."

"And he was home at the time of the shooting?"

"Yes. I personally delivered the news. He was home with one of the twins. She's sick. He didn't take the news well, at all."

I cringed. I wouldn't put anything past him either. I didn't trust him.

"Thank you for coming to tell me."

"Ok. Take care Strawberry."

I sniffled.

"I'm sorry for the things I said Ray," I apologized.

He smiled and made and "X" over his heart.

Before Ray could pull off, Tobias pulled into the driveway.

Ray drove away and just as Tobias got out of the car, I started to swing on him.

"What did you do to her you bastard! What did you do?"

"What? What are you talking about?"

I was crying and screaming and trying to hit him as hard as I could. My belly was in my way, but a few of my licks managed to reach his face. My neighbors started to come outside and Tobias tried his best to get away from me.

"You tried to kill her!"

"What? Who?"

He was trying to play stupid. I was sure that he had something to do with what happened to Shelly. I was sure of it. Crying, I stood still to catch my breath.

"Where were you?"

Tobias opened his car doors, and walked around to the trunk. The car was filled with baby stuff. He'd gotten everything from a crib, to a car seat. Clothes, diapers, bottles and more.

"I have been shopping for the baby all day. I got everything I could think of. I've been to at least ten stores for the last few hours."

He always has an alibi.

Without responding, I walked into the house, grabbed my purse and my keys and headed back out the door.

My sister needed me. Tobias or Brian deserved to be lying in that hospital bed, not her.

"Where are you going?"

"None of your business. Then again, I'm sure you'll end up finding out."

"What was that about?"

"What?"

"Why was he here?"

"Because unlike him, husband, he's welcomed here!"

I headed to my car, but Tobias spoke behind me.

"Whatever the two of you are planning to do, I wouldn't if I were you," Tobias said.

"What?"

"You heard me. It's in everyone's best interest if he minds his own business. And you should too," he warned and he started getting the stuff out of the car.

What the hell does that mean?

****

Chapter EIGHT

"Come on Shelly baby, wake up."

I hadn't left the hospital in three days. And neither had Shelly's husband Brian. He seemed as though he was taking it pretty hard, but he was faking. At least that's the way that it looked to me. I replayed Shelly's voicemail over and over again.

What did she find out?

Whatever it was, it had to be big, otherwise this wouldn't have happened. I was sure of it.

She looked so peaceful.

The doctors said that they didn't know whether she would make it or not. She wasn't breathing on her own and for now, she was on a breathing machine, but we were hopeful. All that we could do was pray, watch and wait.

"I'm going to find whoever did this to you. I won't rest until I do. And I will make them play. I promise."

And I meant exactly what I said. No more playing nice. It was time to get dirty. I'd done the unthinkable before with crying rape, so I was sure that I could come up with something just as low and grimy as I had before.

Nobody messes with my family. Nobody.

After everyone begged me to go home and get a proper nights' rest, I headed to my house, hoping that Tobias had disappeared.

I'd told Ray that Tobias had said that he was baby shopping all night and after narrowing down a few baby stores in the area, sure enough, at the time that Shelly was shot, Tobias was on camera, at *Children's Place*, throwing baby clothes into a cart.

But just because he wasn't the finger behind the trigger, doesn't mean that he didn't know who had pulled it. No one could convince me that it was random. I would never believe it.

I was constantly thinking about all of the things that Ray had told me. He was sure that Tobias had been the man in those pictures, and he was positive that he'd gone by different names, with previous wives. I believed him. Unless they were identical triplets, with crazy different names, and Tobias just forgot to mention it, but I doubted it. It was Tobias.

And I couldn't help but wonder what plan he thought that he had for me. But little did he know that I was about to cancel Christmas on his ass. I had a meeting with my lawyer later on this week, and I was proceeding with the divorce. I'd told him everything that I knew, and he had a few ideas to make sure that I came out on top.

Arriving home, his car was in the driveway.

I'd applied for a gun permit that I'd gotten back the day the same day that Shelly was shot, so instead of going in, I pulled off and drove to the gun store downtown.

I didn't trust Tobias and I had to be prepared just in case he tried something crazy.

I hadn't talked to him the whole time that I was at the hospital. He called and texted to check on the baby, over and over again, but I never responded. I was sure that if he hadn't seen what happened to Shelly on the news that his little friend Brian probably filled him in.

After getting something small, something that I could handle, I headed back home. Of course I knew how to use it. Ray had taught me years ago. And it would make my heart smile to have to send Tobias to an early grave. It would be my absolute pleasure, so he had better leave me the hell alone. But arriving home, this time, Tobias's car was gone.

Heading inside, the scent of bleach and other cleaning supplies, almost made me nauseous.

The house was spotless. Everything was cleaned. Walking around the entire house, he'd cleaned everything, and even washed and folded the laundry.

On my way to my bedroom, I noticed that the spare bedroom across the hall had a blue ribbon on it, so I pushed open the door.

"Aww," though I didn't want to like it, I loved what Tobias had done with the room. He'd turned it into the baby's nursery. He'd set up the crib, changing table, a walker, a swing. He even had a futon decorated against the wall, just in case I decided to sleep there. I looked at the rocking chair. The rocking chair had a plush little bear sitting on it, which made me smile.

"Do you like it?"

I jumped and turned around with an attitude.

"Don't sneak up on me like that!" I hadn't even heard Tobias come in.

"Can we talk?"

I shut the door to the nursery and headed towards the living room.

"What?"

"How is your sister?"

"As if you really care. What do you want to talk about?"

I held my purse close to me, just in case I had to pump his ass full of lead. I'd loaded the gun in the car so I was ready.

"What do you know?"

"About?"

"What has you little officer ex-husband told you?" Tobias asked.

"I don't know what you're talking about."

I felt that maybe playing dumb was my best option. Hell from the looks of it, someone had shot my sister to keep her quiet, so, I was going to act like I didn't know anything important.

"Fine. If you don't want to be honest, neither will I."

He glared at me and I stared back.

"Okay, I know Tobias isn't your real name."

"Correct."

So he really was going to be honest?

Okay. Let's keep going.

"What is your real name?"

"You tell me."

"I also know that you have been married twice before."

"Only twice?" he chuckled.

My goodness, how many wives had he had?

"So, I was just what? Something to do?"

"No. You were an opportunity."

I felt myself getting angry but I knew that if I flipped out, he would probably shut down.

"An opportunity for what?"

"To do what we always do."

He said we. So, he and Brian must have had some type of plan from the very beginning.

"And what's that?"

"It doesn't matter. The problem is that I haven't done my part. I always do my part. And then I saw him, our son, my son, and I just wanted to be a part of his life. I wanted to be his dad. I wanted to be the dad that I never had."

"Wait, I thought your parents were married."

"My mother is doing life in prison and I never met my father. Those folks that you spoke to were friends. They owed me a few favors."

He just lied about everything!

So that's why none of his "family" made it to the wedding. He didn't have any.

"What are you saying Tobias?"

"I'm saying that I have to come up with a plan. We have to come up with a new plan."

"What do you mean we?"

"Like I said we."

"I have nothing to do with whatever you are talking about."

"Trust me. You have everything to do with it."

I started yelling at him and telling him that I hated that I ever met him and that he was the worst mistake of my life. I told him that he could take his plan and shove it up his skinny, black ass!

I didn't know what he was involved in and I didn't care what happened to him. I just wanted him out of my life. And I wanted him out now!

"Why can't you just go? Please just go."

"I'm not leaving behind my son. I just can't."

"He won't miss, who he doesn't know. If you leave now, he won't know you, and he will be just fine."

"I can't leave him. He's my second chance."

Huh?

"I had a son once."

"What?"

"I had a son."

"Had? I thought you said that you didn't have any kids Tobias."

"I don't. But I did."

I stared at him as he stared off into space.

"I took my eye off of him for a second. One little second. He was two years old and curious. I was the one that wanted the house by the lake. I was unloading the truck. I took my eye off of him. When I turned back around, he was gone. I checked the house, hoping that maybe he had gone inside but he wasn't there. My heart skipped a beat as I headed to the backyard. I saw his little hand come up out of the water as if he had been trying to swim. So I went running. I still remember how bad my eyes burned as I looked for him in the water. I found him, but I was too late. I tried to bring him back, but I was too late."

I fought back tears. I couldn't imagine. I had no idea. Why wouldn't he have told me something like that?

"Where was his mother?"

"She wasn't there. But she never fully forgave me for it. But I couldn't bring him back and I didn't want to replace him either. So, I refused to get any woman pregnant again. I always used protection, and then, I made the mistake with you. I was trying to fix it. I was hoping that you lost it, every single day. But you didn't. And now that he's coming, it just changes some things. Not all things, but some."

"Why are you telling me all of the Tobias? Why?"

He took a deep breath.

173

"Because if I don't figure out something…"

"What?"

"If I don't figure out a plan Tiffany…you're going to die."

What?

I looked at his face and he looked as though he was sure of it.

Die? How, why, was I going to die?

Just as I opened up my mouth, the lights flickered, and then they clicked off. The house was dark except the light from the moon shining in over the front door, making the room visible.

"Oh shit. She's here," Tobias said, as he walked closer to me.

"What? Who's here?" I asked as he grabbed my hand.

Out of nowhere, I heard what sounded like a chainsaw and then I watched it come through the front door, just above the door knob.

What in the hell?

"Who's here Tobias? Who's here?"

"My wife," he said, grabbing my hand and pulling me in the opposite direction.

What? What the hell did he mean *his wife*?

****

TO BE CONTINUED…

PART TWO OF "THE HIDDEN WIFE" DROPS AUGUST 26TH, 2014. MARK YOUR CALENDARS, OR JOIN MY FACEBOOK GROUP FOR SNEAK PEEKS AND MORE BY CLICKING HERE:

https://www.facebook.com/groups/authorbmhardin/

IF YOU ENJOYED THIS BOOK, BE SURE TO DOWNLOAD MY NEWEST RELEASE "THE GOOD LISTENER" BY CLICKING HERE:

https://www.amazon.com/Good-Listener-B-M-Hardin-ebook/dp/B01HTWZPME/ref=sr_1_1?ie=UTF8&qid=1469680283&sr=8-1&keywords=bm+hardin

Author B.M. Hardin's contact info:

Facebook: http://www.facbook.com/authorbm

Twitter: @BMHardin1

Instagram: @bm_hardin

Email:bmhardinbooks@gmail.com

TEXT BMBOOKS to 22828 for Release updates!

List of Author B.M. Hardin's best sellers:

Your Pastor My Husband

The Wrong Husband Part One and Two

Reserve My Curves

Desperate: I'll Do Anything for Love

Check out any of these reads by clicking here:

https://www.amazon.com/s/ref=nb_sb_noss?url=searc
h-alias%3Daps&field-keywords=bm+hardin

Made in the USA
Charleston, SC
14 November 2016